THE RESISTANCE AND THE EMPIRE

The Dream World Trilogy #3

Michael A. Susko

AllrOneof Us Publishing
Baltimore, Md & Huntsville, Al

This is a work of fiction. Similarities to real people, places, or events are entirely coincidental.

THE RESISTANCE & THE EMPIRE

First edition. August 14, 2021.

ISBN: 979-8201296407

Written by Michael A. Susko.

To those who resist to create a better world.

CHAPTER I
A FEELING

The late August flowers were in bloom, and there was a sense of deep lushness among the plants. Despite the relaxation of the garden, Detinna decided to bring up something that had been bothering her. "It seems like we got all we've wanted. We're happily married. We're thinking about having kids. But I can't help thinking the Watchers will find us one day."

Delphi tried to offer reassurance. "Unlikely. We have a new location, new papers, and we're not going anywhere near the Time Expansion House."

Detinna went over an old argument. "For a Special Unit to disappear--and they think we're responsible—means we're high priority."

"That's over two years ago, and nothing's happened yet. The Resistance has been thorough in their assistance. I'm still amazed at how much they helped us, without us having to join them."

"It's a feeling I have. We need to move to make sure we're safe."

Delphi was surprised. "If we move again, won't it attract attention? The best thing to do is to lie low where we are and live quietly. We've already done our good deed for the world."

"Haven't you been reading the papers lately? There are special camps now for dissenters. They routinely use 'harsh interrogation' which amounts to torture, and there's no other real power than the Ruler. No one seems to care."

"What can we do about it? If we try to speak out, we'll be put on the Watch List. If too many instances and anomalies arise, it will invite an identity check. If they run a DNA or a retinal scan on me, I'll be detected, and we'd likely end up in prison for the rest of our lives."

"We could explain. Maybe they'd—"

"What would we tell them? They wouldn't believe half of it, or if they did, they'd try to recruit us."

"But sitting tight is no plan. I've got a really strong feeling. If we stay here, they're going to find us."

"What do you suggest?"

"We go on the road in a week. Leave our jobs."

"Tell me, what got this all going? Did you have a dream or something?"

"No, not that. Remember, when we risked making a call to the Time Expansion House? Dr. Burgess made a point of saying that they're still looking for us."

"Yes, I remember when I tried to explain what happened in Guatemala, he said, 'You better not tell me.' Instead, we talked about his fantasy vacation at St. Thomas island. I wished we could go on a vacation like that."

"We shouldn't have contacted him. I have a feeling that he sometimes plays both sides, as long as it helps to keep his project going."

"I didn't give any clue to our location, and all our files have been erased."

"There's always something. We've got to move before they find us."

Delphi reflected. "I'm not sure, but I have a feeling that you might be right this time. If we move, where to?"

"I haven't thought that far ahead. Let's start packing.

CHAPTER II
A DREAM LEFT BEHIND

"I find it odd packing and not knowing where we're going," said Delphi.

"I think the key is to leave, not so much where. That will come to us. Maybe there won't be one place in particular."

"You mean stay on the run? We'd need help and money for that."

"If push comes to shove, we could contact the Resistance. They've helped us thus far without making demands."

"You're not thinking of joining? We'd be guaranteeing the worst if we're captured."

"I think our necks are already pretty far out," said Detinna. "If we're going to have a real future—just think—things will have to change."

"Well, speaking of things. I've had success transferring our money to a more accessible account. We can withdraw sufficient funds in three increments. I'm still a little nervous about carrying all that cash."

"We don't have much choice. We're lucky there's still cash in our society. A few more years and all transactions will be completely electronic and traceable."

"You know," said Delphi suddenly. "If we had a child, we wouldn't be doing all this. You'd be playing it conservative."

"Look. The miscarriage was bad enough. It's too much stress wondering if there's going to be a knock on the door."

"On the run, there'll be even more stress."

"Maybe we'll find somewhere that's safe."

"Maybe ... But what happens when our money runs out?"

"There are still jobs under the table. One step at a time, Delphi."

Packing the bags seemed to be the hardest part. Delphi had said if they were going to be on the move, they'd need to travel ultra-light. Ideally no more than three bags. They had compromised at four. Delphi insisted that the load include two backpacks for camping gear and provisions for being on foot.

Notice had been given to their jobs. The day they had to leave was five days away.

Two days later, Detinna woke up and said, "We've got to leave *today*."

"Yes?" asked Delphi, sleepily. "Aren't there some loose ends? I need to cancel memberships and the trash...."

"No time. We got to leave this morning."

"Did you have a dream or what?"

"No, but the feeling is coming back, and it's really strong this time."

"O.K., I've been trusting you on this one. What do you want for breakfast?"

"No time. Pack the electric car. We need to be out of here within the hour."

"Well, I suppose we can do that. Two of the bags are already in the trunk. Just some toiletries. I still hate leaving the aircar behind."

"We've been through that. They'll be expecting us to be running with one, not an archaic car that senior vacationers use."

One hour later, the couple pulled out. Delphi sighed. "Not even a cup of coffee.... Oh, I forgot, we didn't turn off the air units. You know the bill will keep accumulating."

"We can't turn back now. Besides, there won't be any bills, for we won't have any forwarding address," said Detinna.

They hadn't gone more than ten minutes when Detinna started and said, "I forgot something. I can't believe it. We've got to go back."

"What is it? It can't be that important."

"My diary."

"I know you did some writing, but I thought you tore it up after each day."

"Usually I do. But the last entry I recorded was a dream about the Time Thief. I think I revealed too much. We've got to go back."

"Alright," said Delphi.

They were about to turn on their street when Delphi veered away.

"What is it?" asked Detinna.

"They're already there."

"I didn't see anything."

"Two men by the side of the house. A strange vehicle across the street. Eventually, they'll realize we're not home. Thank God we left the aircar there and the power on."

Delphi pressed on. "This car will be hot once they do some checking. I'll give us twenty minutes, max. If we make the expressway fast and put some distance between us and them, then we'll pull off a side road, where there are no camera checks. We have maybe an hour."

Delphi got on the expressway, speeding just above the legal limit. After ten minutes, he pulled off on a side road, then went the other way.

"You're backtracking."

"They'll have photographed us going the other way. Might throw them off for an hour more."

"Where do we go now?"

"There's a nature preserve three hours away. If we can make it there, we'll ditch the car in a secluded area, then walk a few miles and set up camp."

"Camping sounds like fun," said Detinna.

"Trouble," said Delphi abruptly. "There's a security vehicle two cars behind us. We'll try to outrun him if we have to. I don't think they've identified us yet. Their scanners will be running their standard check if we come into view. What bad luck."

Delphi turned into a neighborhood, and the officer turned with him. Still, there were no warning lights to pull over.

"Don't panic. The longer he stays with us, the higher our chances. I've got to pull off."

Delphi pulled into a residential drive, and the officer moved on. No doubt he noted where they pulled in.

Delphi quickly turned around and headed back for the highway. "We don't have much time. When he gets the alarm, our tag and location will be scanned into Central."

They reached the ramp to the highway, and Delphi glanced back. The patrol car was already speeding on the road below them toward the highway.

Delphi gunned it. "We're out of here! We'll get an automatic speeding ticket, but like you said, we won't be home to receive it. Hopefully, we'll be out of sight by the time he reaches the expressway. He won't know which we way we went. It's a fifty-fifty chance."

"Get off the first exit?"

"No, the third. I think we have enough of a jump."

Finally, they pulled off without sighting the officer.

"We're really hot now," said Delphi. "They'll cordon off a ten-mile radius. Time to switch tags."

Delphi pulled over and slid out the car's ID tag, and inserted a new one.

"Where did you get that?" asked Detinna.

"Oh . . . one of the company's vehicles is being repaired."

"Say goodbye to ever driving a vehicle again."

"Small crimes," said Delphi. "We won't make it out of here without another number."

Delphi went up to a parked car, took off its tag and put their old tag on it. "It will inconvenience the people, but it will distract the authorities a while longer."

"Now, you've done two illegal things."

"The list will get longer. Still, we've only bought a little more time before they figure things out."

Delphi went along a back way, which made the going slower, but was less likely to have a roadblock. They passed a routine photographic station and went on.

"I guess we still have an hour or two. We have a shot at reaching the preserve undetected. Get ready to put on your hiking boots."

"Won't they search everywhere? They won't let nature stop them. They'll use dogs."

"No, that's just in the old movies. It's the satellites we have to worry about. I've been studying evasive techniques lately. We need to stay under forest cover for three days, got into the open when there's cloud cover and wear this."

Delphi handed Detinna what looked like a camouflage cape.

"What's that?"

"Thermal insulation. Should fool the heat sensors."

"Where did you get that?"

"I don't know. The jackets were sent to me."

"I think you know who," said Detinna.

Delphi changed the topic. "By the way, I've been meaning to ask you about your dream. What did you put in the diary that was left behind?"

"It was about the power behind the Time Thief. The dream gave me its name. They might call in a psychic and try to call on it."

"Why do you think the dream gave you the name?"

"I don't know. A name gives you some power and control. Maybe it's to help us fight it one day. Or maybe, we'll be tempted to use its power."

Delphi looked her in the eye. "That's one thing I know. We'd never go over to the other side."

CHAPTER III
VANCE AND CLARE

Detinna's face was crisscrossed with distress. "I can't believe you're sinking our car."

They watched as the last of the car bubbled into the lake. Some boats were fishing on the far side of the lake, but they were too distant to have noticed them.

"Lucky for us it's overcast," said Delphi. "In the satellite photos, the car will be seen by the lake, then gone. Not so unusual."

"So that's why you drove all around the lake. If they try to search underwater, they'd have a lot of places to choose from. You've really thought this through," Detinna complimented, "even the camping gear. Still, I hate leaving so many things behind. I don't have half of my toiletries."

"Think of it as going natural," said Delphi. "Relying on your natural bacterial flora."

"I draw the line somewhere. I brought my deodorant and I hope you brought yours."

"Too many chemicals. My saline solution kills bacteria and leaves no smell."

"I've got a feeling we'll both be smelling before this is over."

"You and your feelings," said Delphi.

The couple were still lingering at the spot when a sporty electric compact drove up and another couple stepped out.

"It's good to see some people out here, besides us, roughing it," said a broad-shouldered man who looked like he spent a lot of time outdoors and was good natured.

The middle-aged couples exchanged pleasantries.

Delphi wanted to keep the encounter as short as possible. The more they talked, the more information the other couple might provide if questioned. The man didn't seem to notice that Delphi responded curtly. No names had been exchanged, and Delphi preferred it that way.

"You must be a way from your car," said the man. "We didn't see one along the way. I suppose you're in better shape than us."

"It's nicer view on foot," Delphi said, becoming wary.

"Agreed," said the man.

Delphi looked toward Detinna and noted that she had struck up a conversation with the woman. It wasn't part of the plan. He wanted to warn her. He signaled with his eyes that it was time to leave.

Detinna returned with a questioning look.

The man's companion invited them. "Our camp isn't far from here. Would you like to have lunch?"

"I think we'll be walking some more for the view," Delphi responded.

Detinna hated unilateral decisions. "You haven't asked me, Delphi. I'm hungry and our vehicle is not that accessible."

"We could drive you there?" offered the man.

"No, not necessary," said Delphi. "We — "

The conversation was interrupted by a big air bubble that surfaced out of the water with a loud plopping sound.

"Strangest thing," said the man, staring at the water. Delphi noticed there were fresh tread tracks near the water's edge.

"Maybe, we can join you," Delphi suddenly said, seeking a distraction. "We need to eat, and you've probably got better grub than us."

The man turned from the lake. "Good. My wife has been complaining about not having any company. My name is Vance. Vance Turner. This is Clare, my wife."

"Anne and David," said Detinna, careful enough to use pseudonyms.

Vance hit a button and two seats projected from the back, and the car overhang neatly expanded to enclose them. "Sorry, they're not regular seats, but comfortable enough."

Delphi and Detinna climbed in and they were soon speeding down the lake side.

"I don't know about this," mouthed Delphi.

"They're harmless. The woman was telling me about her favorite recipes."

"We don't know anything about them."

"They're just a vacationing couple. Besides, the Watchers will be looking for two people, not four."

"We don't know anything about them," Delphi repeated. "They could be informants."

"Even if they are, they're not listening to the alerts out here. Let's see what happens."

"OK," said Delphi. "But I have a feeling this time we're going to be surprised."

"Sure, were good pancakes," Delphi complimented. "And the coffee. You've got good stuff."

"We may rough it," said Vance, "but we like good food and coffee."

It was comfortable, almost too comfortable. Vance and Clare had a yellow six-person tent with a polygon design. It looked a lot more comfortable than their small two person emergency tent. They had a shade tarp strung between trees under which they sat at a fold-out table. After ditching civilization, Detinna and Delphi had better food and company than they had in a long while.

Delphi found himself changing his mind about the situation and thinking, *Too bad we'll have to leave soon.* He looked over to Detinna, who was examining a quilt Clare had made.

There was a sudden updraft and low, swirling clouds had dark undertones. "Looks like rain," said Vance. "What are your plans?"

"More hiking and camping, I suppose," Delphi answered.

"Are you taking the Ring Trail or going to the meadow?"

"We'll just see where inspiration takes us," said Delphi, who hadn't heard of either. "We tend not to plan so much from home." He regretted mentioning home, for he didn't want to be queried about the world they had left. Who knows what Detinna had already said. He quickly asked Vance about their plans at the preserve.

"We're vacationing for a couple of weeks. Our strategy is to find a beautiful place, then take our time to enjoy it. Let go of the world and its troubles. We're in no hurry."

Delphi wondered whether the man was recently retired, or independently wealthy, or still working. But he didn't ask what the man did, lest the question be returned.

Detinna came over. "Clare's invited us to stay longer. We're in no hurry to make our hikes, are we?"

Delphi didn't answer right away. "You two have been talking up storm. What's the topic?

"About her family and quilting. They have two grown children, a son and a daughter."

At that point Vance came over and offered another cup of coffee. He had heard the last sentence and added, "Yes, and we're happy to say they both have jobs."

"What do they do?" asked Delphi, breaking his rule about asking for personal details.

"Our daughter's in business, and our son works for the government."

"The government?"

"He's an officer in the security forces, but he doesn't do hard core stuff. Just analyzes data."

Delphi, trying to hide his expression, said a little stiffly, "You must be proud of them."

"We are. We're hoping they'll find spouses next."

A hike was proposed. Detinna and Delphi washed up and had a moment together. "I think it's time we ditched them," said Delphi. "Their son's in security. If he happens to call them, we might be mentioned. We need to move on and create as much distance as possible."

"Do you really think that they're going to be calling their grown son every day on their vacation?"

"I don't want to take that chance. After the hike, we should go on," insisted Delphi.

Detinna nodded, but her look was downcast.

The foursome went around the lake to the far side. The area ahead of them came alive with the escaping movement of herons and egrets, and other small water birds. "It's so beautiful," Detinna kept saying.

Delphi was absorbed by planning. Where would they go next? Should they stay in the preserve any longer?

Suddenly, Delphi heard a faint whirring and observed a drone flying over the lake. He kept walking forward as if nothing had changed. No doubt they had been surveyed. But they were four, and the distance and angle were such that it wasn't likely that they could make face identification. Detinna was right. They were better off with the other couple as long as they were in the park. He began to think of a cover story, but their stories must match. If Detinna or Ann weren't spending all her time with Clare like she was with a long-lost friend....

A half hour later, Delphi finally got a chance to talk alone with Detinna.

"You what?" he asked.

"I told her you were an aquatic biologist."

"But I don't know anything about fish . . . What else did you say?"

"That we've been married five years and have two children. They're at summer camp."

"Did you have to do that? Don't you understand, the more you tell, the easier it's going to be to say something that will trip us up. I was thinking of staying with them a little longer, but this is becoming even more impossible."

"Sorry," said Detinna. "It felt so natural."

"What were the names of the kids?"

"Zoe and Francis."

"At least Vance doesn't seem to be the prying type. Sometimes, though, I think he sees right through us."

After circling the lake, the couples reached the encampment. Delphi was undecided about what to do for the night. They had agreed to dinner, but where would they go in the dark to set up their small tent? Vance was busy making a fire. Clare had already invited them to stay the night. They hung two extra hammocks in trees, which would be more comfortable that what their thin pads would provide. Amid the tall trees, the lake filled with the orange, setting sun.

Delphi confided to Detinna. "I guess it's the path of less resistance. We'll need to leave though first thing in the morning There's a little-visited rocky portion of the preserve. There should be places to hide."

"Hiding in the rocks? Isn't that what they'd be expecting us to do? I think it's best to hide in plain sight."

Delphi hated to be corrected. "What do you propose? Spend our vacation with these two."

Detinna was silent.

Just then, a transmitter sounded. Vance picked up and started talking. It sounded like family. He spoke for a few minutes, then gave the device to his wife.

It was hard to keep calm. At any moment they might be alerted. But Vance or Clare didn't show any sign that things were wrong.

A little later, Delphi decided to start a conversation. "How's the outside world doing?"

"Oh, that was our daughter. Small stuff. She could be having a major crisis and not tell us until after it's over. But a decision on what type of dress to buy—she calls on our vacation."

It seemed natural enough, but Delphi sensed that the man wasn't telling all. Then again, why should he tell them all about his family matters? First thing in the morning, they would have to leave.

Delphi and Detinna rose early. The other couple were also up early and had already packed.

"We're going to head out," Delphi announced over coffee.

"Oh," said Vance, "which way?"

"The meadows."

"We're going that way. We could drop you anywhere you want along the way. It's a long trek."

"It's alright," said Delphi. "We need the exercise."

The man was about to say something more, then held back.

They had just finished some toast and eggs when the transmitter rang again. "Two calls in two days?" Clare exclaimed. "What could it be? Let me take this."

As she listened, genuine alarm showed in her face. She hung up and said, "They're coming."

"Who's coming?" asked Delphi and Detinna in the same breath.

"The trackers."

"What? You informed on us!" accused Delphi

"No way," said Vance. They could hear the sound of distant rotors. "We wouldn't have told you about it, if we had."

"Get in the car. We haven't much time."

"Who are you?" asked Delphi.

"I think the question is more, who are you. Security is on high alert. They caught your faces somehow and are coming to the lake."

"We're just here on a getaway."

"You can tell the truth later," said Vance. "We knew you were on the run, ever since you sunk your car in the lake. But there's no time for talking now."

Delphi heard the rotors getting louder. He nodded to Zoe. "We are good as cooked if we don't move fast."

They piled into the vehicle.

"Why are you helping us?" asked Delphi as the car sped off.

"We're from the Resistance," said Vance.

CHAPTER IV
THE CORDON CLOSES

The vehicle went surprisingly fast for a ground car. It must, Delphi realized, be fueled by a high octane fuel. It would still be no match for a security vehicle.

Vance leveled off his speed, and Delphi asked, "So you saw us sink the car?"

"No. I only added two plus two. Car tracks led right up to the water, and then the bubble from your sunken vehicle. You two were standing right there. Not usual for someone to ditch their mode of transportation while on vacation. We knew you must be running from someone, and people don't usually run from the Resistance."

The Resistance, pondered Delphi. It was better than the authorities, but not much better in terms of risk. Still, there was not much choice at this point.

Delphi observed Detinna's face, which held a measure of upset, for her newfound friend might have had ulterior motives. But what could she have said? "Hello, we're members of the Resistance. Welcome."

The road was bumpy as the car sped into a forested region that canvassed over them. Vance suddenly stopped the car and said, "We get out here."

"On foot?" asked Delphi.

"Just a short distance."

Vance set some instructions on the car's computer, and the empty car sped ahead. "It will use its GPS to track the road for a good distance, then I've programed the car to wreck."

The trackers would be fooled, but for only a short time, thought Delphi.

With Vance in the lead, the group walked into the dense forest and came to a mound of green boughs. A second vehicle was revealed that looked sleeker, faster, and had a hidden, recessed compartment for two in the back. "Women in the back," said Vance. "We're going fishing."

Delphi and Detinna looked at each and shrugged.

The vehicle rode surprisingly well off road, as Vance steered closer to the lake and greater visibility.

The car didn't stop when they reached shore. Detinna and Delphi both gasped as they entered the water. The top of the car popped open, a propeller extended from the car's underside, and their boat sped along.

Vance pulled out some portable rods from a side compartment. "Time to go fishing," he said after stalling the engine. Nearby, two other boats were doing the same.

Vance set up the poles and tossed the line out.

"No bait?" asked Delphi.

"No, but we have some beer. Kick your feet back. Here's a hat."

Ten minutes later, a plane-helicopter passed overhead. "Wave," said Vance.

"Won't they check us out, if we're within the search cordon?" asked Delphi.

"Won't be the first thing they do. After they find our first vehicle and no tracks leading away, they'll have to back track the whole length of the road."

There was a sudden increase in sounds in the distance. Several crafts were circling their former encampment. The entire area would soon be swarming and cordoned off. It looked like they would be caught in the security net, after all.

Vance, seemingly oblivious, pulled up on his rod a few times. "Well, no luck," he said. "Maybe we should try for a better spot. Buckle in."

The rods collapsed, the top swung over them, and Vance hit the pedal.

The boat-car roared and went amazingly fast.

Maybe, thought Delphi. *We'll make it outside the cordon before it closes off.*

The perimeter was focused on cars on the other side of the lake. Their vehicle gained the road on the far side and was soon speeding up a mountain range.

"Good job," Delphi complimented.

"Contingency planning," Vance replied. "By the way, I was wondering why you came here. If you're running, didn't you know it was a matter of time before they searched the preserve?"

"I figured that it was so vast and that we had three days."

"Normally yes. But it looks like you're high profile. More like a day or two max. Can you tell me, how is it that *you* two warrant such a search?"

"Can't say that we really did that much. Just the opposite, in fact. We've been trying our best to avoid doing anything that would make us stand out."

Vance waited a few moments. "I realize you're just getting to know us. After all, this could be an elaborate plan to recruit you."

"It's doubtful you'd be hanging out in preserve just waiting for us," said Delphi.

"Even on vacation, members of the Resistance are alert to people fleeing from the authorities."

Suddenly, a road block appeared in front of them.

"I'll handle this," said Vance. He slowed the car to a stop as the security official came up. Delphi witnessed Vance undergo a personality change. He was gay, and Delphi was his partner. They had gone to the park for a visit. The security official didn't hide his disapproval, but when he saw the high-level security card that Vance flashed, he waved them through.

Delphi breathed easier. "I thought he'd search our car for sure."

"He should have. But I introduced an extra element to throw them off. Plus, they were looking for a man and a woman. Last, having an Internal Affairs card helps out."

"I'm surprised the cordon went out this far out."

"I think that was just standard security during a heightened alert for special cases. But going back--you must have really done something on your last *mission*. Did it happen to have anything to do with that missing Special Forces team in Guatemala last year? Your wife mentioned to Clare that you've traveled to Guatemala."

"She did?" asked Delphi, plainly annoyed.

"I know you don't look like the type that can take out an elite team. Maybe you have some powerful friends. You don't have to tell us anything, but I'm hoping that you'll talk to some higher ups and consider joining us. It doesn't seem like you have much future on the outside."

Delphi had no reply and Vance hit a button and a monitor showed the women talking. "Looks like our wives are still friends."

Delphi sensed that his life was changing. He looked at Detinna talking, oblivious to the danger.

Could it be an elaborate ruse? Delphi wondered. *No, it would take too much imagination.* The couple had run into the vaunted Resistance, so notorious that even associating with them could bring a sentence of indefinite detention.

"How did you manage to obtain that high security ID?" Delphi asked. Vance was driving leisurely through winding mountain roads, and the question reminded him of a world that he wished did not exist. The hidden compartment was raised now, and the four were driving like in a convertible.

"It's just paper," answered Vance. "The hard part is making sure the computers on the other end don't flag it."

"You mean you've got people on the inside?"

"We have friends, just as you do," said Vance with a half question in his reply.

Detinna joined the conversation after she got caught up to speed. "I'm afraid you've got it wrong. Delphi and I are not some special agents. We're just ordinary people who got caught up in things."

She wanted to tell more, but hesitated. What could she really say which wouldn't sound crazy? The Time Thief, the other dimension?

Clare sensed her reluctance. "You don't have to tell us anymore. For whatever reason, you're wanted by the authorities. Some other people most likely got you mixed up in this."

Detinna sensed she could trust these people and revealed––despite knowing that Delphi would disapprove. "Yes, it was through a Time Expansion class..."

"Dr. Burgess? Oh yes, he's one of our assets," said Clare, laughing.

"You mean he's part of the Resistance?" asked Delphi.

"Yes and no," Clare explained. "I don't think he lets himself *know*. He's smart enough to work for us, without having to formally announce it. He just steers people a certain right way and well, they sometimes come over."

"Why don't the authorities shut him down? Surely, they've flagged him by now?"

"Well, sometimes he 'works' for them. Just enough, like a low level agent. We tolerate those losses. Our gains are greater."

"You're kidding! He plays both sides?"

"Let's just say he survives, and the good outweighs the bad. But as you can see, he's brought you to us."

"He didn't suggest that we come to the preserve," Detinna protested. "I just had an intuition..."

"Most likely, he implanted a suggestion and sent you a cue. Did you take the latest course on Hypnotic Suggestion?"

"I didn't know that it was offered."

"You're kidding us!" said Delphi, who had been holding in his peace. "What else did he plant in her mind?"

Vance was no longer listening, for a red light was flashing on his console.

"What is it?" asked Delphi.

"Incoming. Brace yourself."

Vance slammed his brakes, skidded into a 360-degree turn, and sped in the other direction. Three seconds later, an explosion ripped the road a hundred yards behind them. The noise was deafening, and the car was jolted forward by the shock wave.

"Didn't expect that," said Vance.

A display console popped open in the back seat. "They're trying to kill us with a manned fighter!" screamed Clare. "That's not protocol."

"Our guests must have made somebody *really* angry," Vance half shouted. "Most likely an errant tracker upset over a buddy who died. Get ready, for he'll swing back around. This car has a few tricks, but an explosion that size will kill us, if we're within fifty feet. If they're smart, they'll blow out the road ahead and behind us."

"We've got ten minutes before we enter a dense forest area," said Clare. "They can get in one more shot, maybe two."

"What do you suggest?" asked Vance.

"Go ten percent slower than your maximum, and after it's fired, see if you can outrun it."

"Too slow, I think. He'll get in another shot and know our maximum speed. Calculate it."

Clare brought out a hand-held device, plugged into a slot in the car, and punched in a few numbers. "One hundred and eighteen kilometers per hour should give you 100 feet from the next explosion."

"Too close. If he shoots slightly ahead like a good gunner, we're toast. Try 110."

"That will give you 150 feet, but you will only have five seconds to spare before he can get off the second."

"OK, 115. Hang on."

It was frustratingly slow, waiting to be locked on. At some points the trail was winding down the side and but for a quick turn, they would end in the lake. *There's no way,* thought Delphi. *He'll have to go much faster.*

"Maybe we should abandon the vehicle, put the car on automatic, and let them blow the car up," suggested Delphi.

"No chance for survival away from the car," Vance replied. "We might live a half hour longer."

The curves were becoming steeper. "You're slowing down too much," warned Clare. "Recalculating. You only have a few seconds to spare . . ."

The console lit up, and Vance hit the accelerator. There was a straight spot, then they slowed into a long curve. The car skidded, but Vance retained control.

He hit the accelerator again, a curve. Then impact.

The missile struck within seventy-five feet. The car was pushed up and forward, then bounced, and landed with a thud, the engines cut off. Everyone inside was stunned. Vance's nose was bleeding. "We'll survive," said Vance, shaking his head. Delphi looked at him speaking, but could hear only faintly.

Delphi turned and saw Clare recalculating. She screamed. "We're minus five seconds. He's got us."

"Not yet," returned Vance.

He pushed full scale on the accelerator around a hairpin curve with the lake below. There was no time.

"You've gained a second," Clare said. "Thirty seconds till the second lock in. No time."

Delphi looked at Detinna. They both said goodbye with their eyes. Detinna put her hands against her temples to protect herself from her eardrums bursting.

A few moments more and Vance's steady voice said, "It's coming in."

"Missile will enter the kill zone," declared Clare.

"It's over," said Delphi, reaching back to hold Detinna's arm.

"Brace yourself," said Vance.

Vance hit the accelerator fully to outrace the missile. *There's no way the car will hold the turn,* thought Delphi.

He was right. The car sailed over the cliff and nose-dived into the lake below.

CHAPTER V
BASE 54

"Brace yourselves," yelled Vance. "Missile, then water."

A fire ball erupted behind them, and a blinding light flared over them. The temperature rose instantly, hot as an oven.

Just as it seemed they would be burned alive, the car slammed into the water, and they were enveloped by darkness. A shock wave shook them, muffled by ten feet of water. The temperature relaxed.

Delphi and Detinna were too stunned to move as the car kept sinking. "We've got to let some water in before the pressure becomes too great," said Delphi, remembering a survival technique.

"Not necessary," said Vance. "We're still functional. Hang on for landing."

Five seconds later, the car thudded into the lake bottom, nose first. The windshield was blackened from a mud burial.

"I can't believe we're alive," said Detinna.

"We survived, barely," Clare concurred. "The water saved us from the shock wave."

"Kept us from burning, too," added Vance.

"Not much better than buried in the mud at a bottom of a lake," said Delphi.

"Like I said, the car is still functional," said Vance. "Let me run a status check."

Vance clicked buttons on from a side compartment in the console. "Systems are still good."

He tested a reverse thruster. The car shook but didn't move.

Vance cursed, then said, "I knew they should have put more power into those thrusters. Let me add reserve power, maximum torque." The car made a slight movement, then none. They were stuck.

Vance and Clare didn't want to say it. For all the technology, they were entombed.

Vance, however, reassured them. "There's usually a way out of things. You're good at this type of thing, Clare?"

She ran some calculations. "Nothing immediate," Clare said after a couple of minutes. "At least we've disappeared from any sensors."

Vance ran the thrusters and auto power together. Still no movement.

They sat in silence for a couple minutes more, then Clare suggested, "We can try rocking with our bodies. If we all sway together, we might loosen in the mud."

They rocked, but the car didn't move.

"Too tight," said Detinna. "Maybe rock and thrust and use auto power at the same time."

This time, there was a little movement.

Inch by inch, the vehicle loosened. Finally, the reverse thrusters alone created movement.

"We're good," said Vance as the car crawled along the bottom. "But we've used up too much fuel. We have only thirty minutes of fuel to get to our destination."

"Where's that?" asked Delphi.

"Nearby," said Vance, keeping purposively vague. "By the look of things, you could use some alternate locations as well." There was a half question in his voice again.

"It's a long story," Delphi replied.

"You know, it's not too late to back out," Vance offered. "We can refuel, then drop you off in a remote region. Call it quits. The Resistance is not for everyone."

"I don't know," said Delphi. "I think we know too much. Where else would we go?"

"Alright," said Vance. He punched in the destination, and the car-submarine snaked along the murky bottom.

"No doubt they're watching above to see if we would attempt a retrieval."

"Is that the depth?" asked Delphi, pointing to a clock with red numbers counting down.

"No, that's the amount of oxygen left."

"It says twenty minutes. Won't we have to surface?"

"I have a plan," said Vance.

Delphi wondered, *What plan could they have for being stranded in the middle of a lake?*

The murk remained thick, and it offered protection.

A warning light came on.

"What is it?" asked Delphi.

"A submersible vessel at the point we entered the lake. They've started the retrieval. "

"How much lead time do we have?" asked Delphi.

"Maybe twenty minutes before they reach us," answered Vance.

Delphi watched as the oxygen clock diminished to fifteen minutes. "Time's running out with O2 as well."

Vance didn't respond. He was focused ahead, as if avoiding some impending obstacle.

"Can't see it yet . . . Proximity transponder must be out," Vance said to himself. "We'll have to manually search."

"You mean, use our eyes?" asked Delphi.

Again, no response, for Vance was intently focused ahead

The oxygen meter read five minutes.

"Are you near the shore?" asked Detinna.

Suddenly, the car bumped into something hard, making a metallic clang.

"Circle around," said Clare. "My calculations show we must be on the North side. Go to the right."

The oxygen meter was approaching zero.

"Don't worry," said Vance. "There's a three minute reserve before we actually run out." Again, another light lit. "Vehicle nearby," reported Clare. "Shall we take it out?"

"No time," said Vance.

Their vehicle headed straight toward a solid object. "It's not opening," said Vance, pressing a button.

"Fail safe procedure. Insert the emergency explosive."

"Here goes," said Vance.

The car fired a harpoon-like object that exploded a dozen feet away. An opening appeared out of nowhere and the car darted through.

The four found themselves in an underwater holding chamber. They could hear the sound of water draining. The air was stifling. Lights came on. The convertible top popped off.

"Where are we?" asked Detinna.

"Emergency retrieval base Number 54," Vance informed. "Over here, quickly."

The two couples climbed into a car that rode on uplifting air from the bottom of the tube. Vance hit a lever. A door closed behind them, and there were sounds of rushing water. Soon they were jetting down a tubed tunnel.

"Quite an elaborate contingency," Delphi complimented.

"In the age of the empire, one doesn't survive long without them," said Vance.

They traveled in silence for thirty seconds before the vehicle slowed and they entered a docking room. Other people were present to greet them. Vance and Clare seemed to be well known. The four were escorted down a hall into a large room with a series of consoles, which looked like a command center. In modules, a dozen people were monitoring informational read-outs.

Detinna and Delphi were amazed.

"All this is underwater, and the computers look as advanced as the state's."

"In a way, it is the state's system," said Vance. In answer to the alarm on Delphi's face, he added, "We've managed to tap into the system up to a certain security level. We have to be careful about not giving away our presence by energy fluctuations. Thus far, they haven't noticed us siphoning information yet. It's worth seeing what they're seeing, even at the lower levels. That's how we managed the retrieval."

"The retrieval?"

"You and your wife," Vance answered.

Delphi looked dumbfounded. "So it was an elaborate operation."

Vance smiled. "When we realized that the state was coming for you, we decided to implant subliminal suggestions. That's Clare's expertise. Detinna is a receptive."

"How did you do it?" asked Detinna.

"I can explain more fully later," said Clare. "But one thing I can say now. You still had a real choice to act on the suggestions or not."

They continued walking through a set of double pressurized doors into a more secure area, protected by guards. In the next area, they were joined by two men who seemed to carry authority. Delphi decided neither one was a superior as they deferred to Vance.

Delphi dropped back to talk to Detinna. "We're getting into this rather thick, now that we know the location of this base. There's not much turning back now, no matter what they say. We know the approximate location of a Command Post for one."

"So what can they possibly be taking us here for? We don't have any experience in Resistance."

"No doubt we're here to meet the leader of the outpost, or maybe even the Leader of the Resistance, " Delphi guessed. "I hope it's not the latter. You've heard the stories."

"The most hunted man in the world, a ruthless terrorist. You know it's mostly propaganda, but even if some of it is true...."

"We're in too far to turn back now," repeated Delphi.

As they passed through another level of security, Delphi and Detinna wondered what would happen when the Resistance found out they were just ordinary folks. True, they had a knack for the other world and they had managed to free the Time Thief against all odds. But the Time Thief had dissolved on his own, they had barely escaped with their own skins, and the Cave God was the one who took the Special Forces unit to their doom. They would explain all this to their leader, and maybe they would be given an identity change, and placed back in society.

The group entered a conference room, sat down, and waited. Delphi was thinking that more powerful people always keep you waiting, when he suddenly became nervous. *They must have something specific in mind for us.* Detinna was having flashes to when she was kidnaped. She observed there was no other door and that the leader would have to enter from the door they came in.

A couple of minutes later a man in his twenties, who carried a briefcase, entered the room. He appeared to be an assistant. Vance took some papers from the man and examined them. Clare scrolled through a small computer device.

Vance looked up and said, "We have a need for everyone's services here."

"I thought we were going to meet the leader of the outpost?" Delphi interjected.

"I'm the leader of the Resistance," Vance revealed. "Although Clare here shares much of the burden."

Delphi doubted him. "What? Isn't it risky for the leader of the Resistance to be retrieving us?"

"Even leaders take vacations, and I used to be an expert in retrieval. Besides, you're a high value asset."

Delphi wondered what was true. It still didn't make sense to risk your most important person to retrieve them.

"We need to tell you something," Delphi went on to say. "We aren't anyone special. About all we've done is make some out-of-body journeys to the other world. Last time, we had to go to Guatemala to do it. We encountered old Mayan gods and escaped by the skin of our teeth. That's it. We can't really shoot a gun or do any fancy black belt stuff. The Special Forces team followed this indigenous chief and never came back again. We don't know what really happened to them. Detinna here will tell the same."

Vance nodded and said, "Our evaluation remains the same. You were able to make a connection to the other world when you needed to. That alone could prove quite useful to us. Equally, if not more importantly, you have a number of allies as well."

"Allies? I'm afraid you're mistaken," said Detinna. "We don't have any powerful friends."

"Ah, but you do," said Clare. "When the Time Thief died and released the years he had stolen, a lot of people's time was returned, in many cases a sizeable number of years. When people with their newfound youth found out that you were the ones responsible, they were quite thankful that you risked your lives to do that. And believe me, word like that gets around."

Detinna looked toward Delphi. "We weren't really aware that other's years would come back. How many are there?"

"Let's say an undetermined number. Michael here is one of them."

"Thanks," said Michael, speaking up for the first time. "I think my wife is more thankful than I am. We had to retrieve you, don't you understand, even if it risked our leader."

"The credit really goes to Detinna," said Delphi. "It was her idea, and I resisted all the way. It was her determination that—"

"We couldn't have done it without each other," said Detinna. "We were both involved."

"No matter how. It was done," said Vance.

"But we had no plans to join the Resistance," said Delphi. "We were just trying to escape and live quietly."

"We are not going to interfere with your choice," said Clare. "But the authorities were about to find you, and we had to ensure that you met us and had an opportunity for assistance."

There was a sudden thud, then another, and everyone looked up. A call came in to Vance.

"They're sending random probes," Vance informed, looking to Clare. "They must have confirmed that the car is missing from the kill zone. How much time do we have?"

Clare did some calculations. "It's hard to say, depends on a two or three unknowns. My guess is a day or two, unless they get lucky."

"How soon could it be if they get lucky?"

Clare did more calculations.

"Well, an hour or two."

Vance turned to Michael. There was a moment of decision, and they both nodded.

"Shut down the systems," Vance ordered. "We evacuate within thirty minutes."

Michael hit a command on his console, and a red light started flashing above the door.

"Sorry, your comforts here are short lived," said Vance.

CHAPTER VI
EXPLOSION FREE FALL

Another thud sounded, slightly closer. "Prepare Pod Four."

"Where are we going?" asked Michael.

"Base Three," Vance replied.

"The base near the capital?" asked Clare.

"We need to make our move soon," said Vance. "All the players are in place."

"A submersible vehicle is ready," said Michael, who was joined by another woman. "This is Tiffany Nelson—explosives, weapons, and survival expert," he introduced.

A shapely woman, festooned with packs, greeted them. Delphi was about to joke about the contrast between her feminine sounding first name and her job, but decided against it. She was carrying, it seemed, enough explosives to blow the center up.

The company walked through a series of chambers. The members of the Resistance were shutting down systems, gathering effects. There were maybe fifty people in all.

"I'm sorry," said Detinna. "We've cost you this base."

"It was only a matter of time before they found us anyway," said Vance. "We might as well leave with some lead time."

Moments later, they were strapped in, and their vehicle ejected.

"How will we get past the cordon this time?" asked Delphi. "Won't the perimeter be in place?"

"We have a plan," Vance answered.

The craft traveled steadily, following the lake bottom for a half hour. Then the vehicle crawled along the shore, staying just submersed. A periscope was raised. A blast was heard in the distance.

"What's happening?" asked Detinna.

"A diversion on the far side," said Vance. "A high-speed vehicle has caught their attention."

"Most likely it will be destroyed," added Clare, "but it should give us the time we need."

"They are willing to die to save us?" asked Delphi.

"All of us are willing. A crew most likely volunteered," said Michael.

"We aren't Scott free yet," added Vance. "Even if we make it outside the perimeter, contact with robotic patrols is likely."

They waited longer as loud explosions sounded, not so distant.

"What now?" asked Detinna, unable to mask her anxiety.

"The enemy is still being diverted," said Clare. "We're waiting for a hole in the surveillance. The gaps are only for a second or two, and we need at least five."

"Nothing doing," said Vance. "We'll have to go with less. Take off from water?"

"It will take too much fuel," said Clare. "We have just enough to reach our site as is."

"If we don't get out of here soon, lack of fuel will be the least of our concerns. We're dead unless we punch through. We have to avoid contact in the immediate area."

"Gaps are now 3.5 seconds," Clare reported.

"Ready, on your signal," said Vance. The craft pointed upwards from the lake bottom and a booster rocket energized.

A monitor droned, "Three, two, one...."

"Hang on," said Vance, punching a button.

The craft vibrated, then roared, and Delphi wondered why they weren't moving. A moment later, the vehicle shot up. The G forces slapped them against their seats as they broke the surface. The vehicle arced toward the ground almost immediately.

Delphi and Detinna wondered if they were going to crash, but the vehicle leveled and skimmed the tree surfaces.

A coded transmission came in.

"Change of plans," said Vance. "The base near the Capital is too hot. There are reports of an intelligence breach. We'll have to go to Back Door."

"Back Door?" asked Michael. "That's not a recorded Safe Site."

"It's an ultra-secret site that only Clare and I know about."

The craft veered a 180 and headed West over the drylands. In a few minutes, they were skimming rock outcrops.

"Mountains in one hour," announced Clare.

"It's maddening, this fast and this close," said Detinna.

Clare explained that it was relatively safe. "The craft has built-in maps and adjusts accordingly. The empire has gotten wise and has erected barriers in random places, but at this speed, we can usually get a visual on them."

Two minutes later, Vance intoned, "Prepare for contact with robotic craft just before Free Space."

Their craft accelerated, and the land below became a blur. "If there is any obstruction, it would definitely come too quickly, but it's a chance we have to take," he added.

The vehicle continued without incident, but warnings flashed. Their craft was tailed.

"How many?" asked Vance.

"Three," said Clare.

"Too many!" Vance exclaimed. "Cover our back side, Tiffany."

The ordinance woman swiveled her chair around, and a small opening with a laser gun popped out.

"What have we got?" asked Clare.

"Not good," Tiffany reported. "Advanced models, and they're triangulating. One on either side, and one's above. Estimated time till lock in, two minutes. Awaiting instructions."

"This is chancy," said Vance. "We'll go straight up. Tiffany, you've got to take out the two behind us, while the one overhead adjusts."

"What about that one?" asked Clare.

"I'm heading for it, a collision course."

"It will let us collide," warned Clare, seeking confirmation.

"Explode option, one to two seconds prior to lock-in."

"Are you kidding? There's no room for error."

"It's the best chance we have," said Vance

"What about activating a bail-out?" asked Michael, wondering why that wasn't considered.

"That will just delay capture. Better to be dead," answered Vance.

Michael uttered an expletive, but Clare was more hopeful, "Alright, let's try it."

Vance activated thrusters, the craft veered, and they launched from midair.

The two side craft fell further behind and sent out small fire ordinance, but it was too distant to be effective. "They're avoiding using missiles, to not take out the craft above," said Clare. "They'll be close enough for lethal regular arms range in ten seconds."

"Permission to send a scatter burst of all our rockets and accelerate just after," called out Tiffany.

"Use all the rockets?" asked Clare.

"It's our best chance for taking both out."

"Go ahead, but save one rocket," ordered Vance.

The rockets were launched in a scatter pattern, and Vance accelerated. A rocket clipped a wing of the robotic ship on the right, disabling it and causing it to spin down out of control.

"One down!" cried Tiffany.

The second robot still bore down on the right side, and their wing was taking direct hits.

"Do you have a shot?" asked Vance.

"It's too close," cried Tiffany.

"Not much time," said Vance. "We'll be disabled in twenty seconds at this rate."

A red flashing light went on, and it was Clare's turn to utter an expletive. "We're locked on. Brace for impact."

"Hang on," said Vance.

A moment later an explosion, and their craft were spinning and falling.

Delphi and Detinna both thought *It's over* and mouthed "I love you." Vance's and Clare's faces were still focused, hands on the controls.

The robotic devices never launched their rockets. The remote controller saw the explosion and assumed that the vehicle from ahead had made the hit. The controller of the vehicle from behind meanwhile assumed that the vehicle above had made the hit and, likewise, diverted his craft.

Their craft was falling and the radius of its fall was calculated. "Send in the clean-up crew. I want all remains for full testing," said the officer in charge.

"We're still spinning. What's happening?" Delphi managed to ask.

"False explosion," Tiffany explained. "The appearance of a hit. But we've got to stabilize before we hit the ground."

Clare's voice held panic. "The hits in the wing are throwing off our attempts to stabilize. I don't how much error to calculate."

"Trial and error," Vance cried.

"We've only got time for five or six tries," said Clare, entering numbers. "There are more than thirty possibilities."

"Intuition, no time to calculate," said Vance. "Forty seconds to impact."

Clare tried three more calculations, all failed. "I thought I had it, but nothing's working," she cried. "We won't make it!"

"You've got to think. You can do it."

Clare tried one more. It didn't work. "There's too much spin. Even if I'm right, I don't think it will work."

"You've got time for another. Fifteen seconds till impact."

"It's not going to work!" cried Clare. "Tiffany, do something."

Tiffany didn't hesitate. She flipped a lever, pressed a button and said, "Brace for shock wave."

Tiffany released the final rocket which exploded on the ground below. It boomed and the aircraft's descent shuddered in the shock wave. There was a moment of semi-stabilization. Clare pressed the last calculation, the aircraft righted, and Vance hit the throttle. The craft spun out of the explosion bloom.

"How was that possible?" asked Delphi, not believing.

Tiffany was all smiles. "Downward projected blast sends an up swell. Anything close would work."

"Why didn't you offer this before?" asked Delphi

"Chances of success are only one in three, and I didn't really think it would work in all the turbulence. It was safer to let Clare take her calculations until we knew it wasn't likely.

"It was cutting it close," said Michael, who had beads of sweat on his neck.

"Good work," said Vance. "From now it should be easy sailing to the Back Door." The craft zigzagged close to the ground over waterless lands, with no sign of habitation. "These places are minimally surveyed," said Michael. "How much fuel do we have?"

"Enough to reach our destination and not much more," Clare answered.

"Mountains ahead. We'll have to climb into Free Space," said Vance. "Should be OK. These places are only occasionally surveyed by robots."

It was clear going. "We're almost there, to the mountain's back side before the rain shadow," informed Vance.

Suddenly, several panels lit up. Vance sounded an expletive.

"What? It's not possible!" exclaimed Clare. "I thought we were in the clear."

"Should we prepare to self-destruct?" asked Tiffany.

"Hold off," said Vance.

"What's going on?" asked Detinna and Delphi at once.

"A fleet is coming straight toward us," said Clare. "We're cooked."

CHAPTER VII
BACK DOOR

"There's not enough fuel for evasive action. We could eject over the mountains," said Clare, grasping for a solution.

"We'd be found, but we'd take a few with us," put in Tiffany.

"Destruct or eject?" asked Clare.

"Neither," said Vance. "Don't touch any buttons. Relax and be sure to wave."

Vance lowered their speed, dropped just under the fleet and continued straight ahead.

"Our transponders should check out, but the protocol is to do a verbal confirmation, then a face check," said Tiffany.

"Not mine," said Vance.

"But you're the leader...."

"Be sure to smile," replied Vance. "Tiffany, change places with Delphi and loosen that vest. I need you up here."

Tiffany moved surprisingly fast, loosening her clothing and wrapping her arms around Vance.

The communicator blipped. Vance turned it on.

"What is your heading? You're close to the fleet," asked the male voice.

Tiffany and Vance turned suddenly, as if just becoming aware of the transmission, and they responded as if tipsy. "We're just out on a pleasure ride, officer," Vance drawled.

"Would you like to join us?" added Tiffany.

The man on the other end laughed as he waited for a face verification. There was a tense moment before the voice said, "Continue on. Just stay outside of fleet radius."

Everyone was relieved, but Clare was surprised at the feelings that arose. "You really seemed to be enjoying yourself," she said.

Vance shrugged. "It's standard diversionary protocol."

"I'm surprised it worked. The odds of escape had gone down to nearly zero."

"How did you escape face verification?" asked Michael, sounding even more surprised.

"Did you see his face?" said Delphi.

"Five points of distortion enough to throw off the age progression," explained Vance.

"Their last photo was over ten years old."

The air-craft landed on a forested mountainside, punctuated by massive rocks. The crew exited and walked up a mountain side where evergreen firs provided a solid canopy.

Two hundred yards away, Vance approached a large free standing rock some two stories high and opened a door. It was Back Door.

Inside, there were three main rooms: a central meeting room with a large one-way window looking out, a kitchen, and a bunk area—all with comfortable furnishings.

"Amazing," said Detinna. "No one else knows about it?"

"The interior was built at a separate location," Vance informed. "It was then airlifted by a crew whom I commanded, and only I knew the coordinates."

"We'll be under blackout for the time being. No communications in or out. Our walls are thermal proof. We're just another rock to any satellite's eye. We should be able to step out occasionally, for the forest cover is heavy enough to avoid visual detection, and we've timed when the telescopic eye is trained this way. We'll wait here till things settle down."

"Won't they realize their mistake in allowing us to pass the fleet?" asked Michael. "Your photo will be rechecked."

"It will take them time, if they piece things together," said Vance. "And all they know is the direction we were traveling."

"But we went in a straight line," said Delphi.

"They'll think it's unlikely we'd simply continue that way," said Vance. "And hopefully we'll be out of here before they do a line check. We're still some two hundred miles down the way."

"We can't even check on the news?" asked Detinna. "Things could drastically change."

"Their detection devices have grown more sophisticated," said Michael. "If we absorb too much energy, it can show as an anomaly. A complete blackout is safest."

"Isn't there a protocol for receiving an emergency transmission?" asked Delphi.

"Not unless we open a channel," said Vance. "But I put out word that we were going to the Black Door. The other cells will know to wait for at least ten days before expecting any major commands. Thirty days on the outside."

"Major commands?" asked Delphi.

"Yes, the time has come for the empire to cease," said Vance. "And we're going to need everyone's help here."

There wasn't much to do at first. Vance and Clare didn't talk about any plans, and most of the time was spent in watching old shows, playing board games, and occasional hikes.

At certain hours they refrained from outdoor activities. When a red light and a beeping came from Vance's watch, they promptly came in.

There was a relaxing half-circle lounge. The one-way glass bay window and dome presented a panoramic of trees and sky. Air from ventilation shafts breezed in.

"The area is surveyed twice a day," Vance informed. "We're in the shadow of the mountain or it would have been four times. There are also rare random checks."

"It would be nice to forget about being watched," said Detinna. "How did it all come to this?"

"It started small," answered Michael, who had an interest in history. "Cameras at intersections to make sure traffic signals were obeyed and cameras on corners of intersections to watch traffic flow. After that, crime-ridden corners with flashing lights and real-time surveillance. Drones were a major step. Now, it's nearly a 100% surveillance system. Add to that a facial recognition system that doesn't produce too many false positives, and routine recording of conversations. In time, you can find questionable material on anyone and use it against them. If all else fails, it's easy enough to falsify digital data, if you need to take out an enemy."

"Has the world actually become safer?" asked Detinna.

"Safer for those who allow their freedom to be taken. But there are always gaps in the system. The Resistance, after all, continues. It seems that humans eventually think of a way around things."

"The worst of it is that crime has become institutionalized by the state," put in Clare. "Pre-emptive invasions, mass detention, torture, outsourcing the worst crimes to private contractors.

"One can't measure the loss in terms of freedom," added Tiffany. "The lost lives, the missed creativity to society."

"I've got to give you credit," said Delphi. "You're willing to put your lives on the line and not just talk about it. We've been just about killed five times since we've been with you."

"And I'm afraid it's because of you," noted Vance. "But it's true. Most people won't take the risk. We don't have the power of the state behind us, but we have each other."

"And we learn to appreciate the times in between," added Tiffany.

"So what's next on the agenda?" asked Delphi.

"Nothing immediate," said Vance. "We have the thirty-day cooling-off period. The system can only be hyper-vigilant for so long. They might even assume, with reduced traffic, that I'm out of action—which I am—and move the search to the back burner."

"It seems disturbing to be totally cut off. Doesn't the Resistance need its leader?" asked Delphi.

"There's back up, if it comes to that," answered Vance. " But we're used to going inactive for long periods. As it is, we're waiting for a few more things to fall in place."

Delphi looked questioningly, but Vance didn't clarify.

"There is something I've been meaning to ask," said Delphi. "If Detinna and I are a part of this plan, don't you think you should tell us what you have in mind?"

"It's a need-to-know and when-to-know basis. If anyone is captured, it's best that they know less than more."

"Maybe after hearing the plan, we can decide whether to go back and live a normal life," said Delphi.

"Yes, you're still free to check out. But the further you go along, the harder it will be to leave."

"We're just escaping with you, basically," argued Detinna. "As for the disappearance of the Special Forces unit—that wasn't our doing. Surely the security forces must realize that by now."

"It's not just that," Michael explained. "The Ruler and his immediate advisors believe you have access to a miracle drug or technique that can make people young again. He won't rest till he that's checked out."

"They'll be disappointed, if they think we've discovered the Fountain of Youth," said Delphi. "But I still can't figure out how you plan to overthrow the entire empire."

Vance gazed steadily at both of them. "I suppose it won't hurt to reveal the outlines of the plan now. If the leader can be incapacitated for even a relatively short period, the entire system can be overthrown. He's amassed too much power to himself. There would be division in the immediate aftermath, and an opportunity for a successful overthrow."

"How will you render inoperative the most heavily guarded man in the world?" asked Detinna.

"Get close to him by convincing him you can give him what he wants most," answered Clare.

The members of the Resistance turned toward Delphi.

"So you think he'll believe that we can give him the goods."

"Yes," answered Vance. "No matter if you actually can or not. It's a way to get close to him."

"And what will I do when I get close to him?"

"Distract him with your offer—we need only a few minutes—and be sure to touch him." "Touch him?"

"The emperor is very suspicious about being touched by someone who's not young," said Clare. "To the point of paranoia, he fears that someone takes his years away. It's mostly psychological. You may not think it will do much. But even a half hour delay, from the center of power during a crisis, can make the difference between the empire surviving or falling."

CHAPTER VIII
THE PLAN

The question remained unanswered, but Delphi felt himself becoming the center of events which were beginning to swirl around him and over which he had little or no control. He wondered how it came to be that he was becoming part of a plot to undo the State and one that would put him directly in touch with the Ruler. No doubt people would die, and he would be indirectly responsible. But wasn't resistance justified? The State, plain and simple, had become a police state. Yes, they were already in too deep, and they knew way too much. Their lots were cast, or were they?

Vance read his hesitation. "You don't have to make a decision now. And this is not the only possible plan. Consider, for a while, and we'll talk again later."

The storm within Delphi quelled for the moment. Vance—who seemed to be able to mind read—wasn't the leader of the Resistance for nothing.

The group had time to get to know one another. Detinna and Clare still talked as if they were old friends. Tiffany and Michael paired up, but it was mostly based on professional interests. Delphi and Vance went out fishing and talked about sports, wildlife and their partners—anything but the plan of operation.

Still, it felt like the calm before the storm, and after a couple of days Delphi became uneasy. Finally, while he and Vance were fishing by a stream, Delphi asked. "I've got to know something. Will I be asked to kill anybody? I don't think I can do that, unless it's self-defense."

Vance weighed his answer carefully. "We aim to minimize death, but death is already occurring daily. Our own death or indefinite detention is what we mostly risk."

Delphi wasn't satisfied. "You're using me to get close to the Ruler. But I'm not an assassin. You have people far better trained than that . . .Tiffany?"

Vance laughed. "We have no assigned roles as assassins. We have missions. People may try to stop us, and we do what is necessary to survive. Your job, as we've said, is only to distract the Ruler during the critical period."

Delphi didn't disguise his frustration. "OK. But what happens to me after the distraction?"

"If he is sufficiently interested, he will talk to you again. But by that time, it should be too late. You, of course, still have a choice in the whole matter."

"You know as well as I do that we're already in way too far over our heads. It doesn't feel like much of a choice."

"We can give you a new identity again."

"I guess them thinking that I'm still twenty years older is a good enough disguise."

The fish suddenly bit. Vance pulled up a large, speckled trout. "Supper," he announced.

After dinner, the group watched a spy thriller. Then Vance decided to break the black out and accept a micro-burst transmission of news.

The lead stories sounded innocuous. No hint of disturbance or heightened alert. But at the end of the news, an image flashed of the most wanted member of the Resistance. An exorbitant reward for information leading to his apprehension was offered. It was an up-to-date photo of Vance.

Vance wasn't surprised.

"How did they know that you're the head?" asked Clare. "And I didn't think they had a recent photo."

"Yes," said Vance, mulling. "The photo was eventually deciphered from when we were checked passing the fleet. As for being the head, they're taking a guess, or we have a high-level leak."

"That's hard to believe," said Michael. "The inner council has been with us for years."

"Maybe one of the council wasn't discreet and told a family member," said Tiffany.

"However it happened, that does change things," said Vance. "From now on we'll have to operate on two tiers. We'll have an inner group. If one of us was the leak, my guess is that we would have been betrayed by now."

"Does that affect our plans?" asked Michael.

"No. The exact plans are still in my head. What has changed is my life expectancy. No doubt they're still conducting an all-out search. It means we'll have to accelerate things, and it's not safe to go outside anymore."

"Maybe we should leave, before they close in," suggested Clare.

"Where to?" asked Vance. "Most likely, any towns along the path of our craft are heavily watched. Nonetheless, our time here is cut short. If they have someone on the inside, it's best to keep moving."

"So where to?" asked Delphi.

"How about a trip to the capital to pay a visit to the Head of State?" suggested Vance.

"Just like that?" asked Clare.

"We could go in two groups. One with me to offer formal negotiations, and the other off the record. It's a matter of time before I get caught, so I can risk offering to meet in a neutral place. It would be a show of strength that we really don't have."

"The second team will be with Delphi, who will dangle the prospect of youth to the Ruler. That will buy time for the others."

"Others?" asked Detinna.

"No need to know, even when things are launched. Specific operational commands are segregated. Everyone does their part, and it will come together."

"What if the others fail?" asked Delphi.

"Then we fail too, but at least we have tried. "

Detinna asked Clare, "You're always calculating the odds. What are our chances of success?"

"There is no one mathematical formula, for there are too many variables. My intuition says it's not bad odds, but not great either. I'd say about a 1 in 3 chance of success. It goes up to 50% with a good diversion. So Delphi evens our odds."

"That's great that things are depending on me," said Delphi. "What are the teams?" Vance nodded. "Clare and I will remain together. Delphi and Tiffany, then Michael and Detinna will stay behind."

Detinna could barely restrain her irritation from being separated from Delphi. "What will we do here?"

"You'll provide back-up operational control. The authorities may ask confirmation regarding Delphi."

"But Delphi and I have always done things together."

"I'm afraid we'll need Tiffany's specific operational skills for this mission. If things don't go as planned, and it's likely that they won't at some point, she's the one who can bring Delphi out alive."

Detinna couldn't argue against that, but she wondered at a plan that would put her husband's life in the hands of another woman. That evening Vance revealed separately the outlines of each group's plan.

The next day, Detinna couldn't help asking Delphi. "You probably don't mind having a young female companion on this mission."

"Hold up, Detinna. You know that this is strictly professional. Plus, it wasn't my choice."

"See, you're not denying it. Tell me, what's the plan with her?"

"You know I can't reveal specifics. Everything will be alright."

"No doubt you'll bond with her. She has that killer figure—in more ways than one. I know how these things can work out."

"Detinna, that's just in the movies. You and I are married and committed to each other, remember? I think the thing we're risking most here are our lives."

"We could call it quits and try our luck again on the outside," Detinna suggested, trying to convince herself. "They would set us up with money and a new identity."

"What our chances then?" asked Delphi.

"Michael says that almost all escape detection for five years, and half never get caught."

"So we might never be caught, but uncertainty will always be hanging over our heads. But if this operation succeeds, we won't have to be calculating odds. We will have changed things. I think we need to make a go of it."

Detinna was still uneasy. "We're really crossing a line this time. Things will never be the same after this, whatever way they go. Something can easily go wrong. One of us will could get captured, and we won't have a future together. I can sense it."

"It would take a lot to separate us," answered Delphi, and he kissed her.

"Alright," said Detinna. "Just know I'll always be waiting for you."

"Of course," said Delphi.

"Have you decided?" Vance asked the next day. Tiffany and Michael were in the room with them.

"I can't say my wife fully approves," said Delphi, "but we're willing to go on this mission."

Vance smiled broadly, and Tiffany complimented, "I knew you would come through. You have it in you."

Delphi looked intently at the both of them. "There's one condition. After it's all over and if we succeed, Detinna and I want to live peacefully and not be bothered by all this again."

Vance paused and Delphi wondered why he had could not easily grant this wish.

"I can only say that you will have that choice," Vance answered. "We'll help you with whatever choice you make, but I can't guarantee what the future will bring and what you will be able to choose."

"Fair enough," said Delphi.

"Good. The training will start right away."

"Training? You mean my cover story?"

"Yes. You will also learn a remote surveillance technique in order to gain credibility. You'll need more than a good story."

"Another out-of body technique?" guessed Delphi. "Things are more unpredictable if we start dabbling in that."

"That's usually the case," Michael agreed.

"Doesn't that require a rather strong bond with your partner?" Delphi said, glancing at Tiffany.

"Yes again. But you're a natural. It shouldn't be hard," said Vance.

"OK.... Any other surprises?"

"Your trainer for other-world access part will be Michael, however. Tiffany has only been recently trained herself."

"I thought you were just a policy wonk, the one who knew all the regs," said Delphi.

Michael's smile showed he wasn't offended. "That alone wouldn't have got me into the inner circle."

After Vance and Tiffany left, Michael remained with Delphi to review their plans. Delphi had some doubts. "A problem with out-of-body experience is that it's sometimes hard to come back."

"True enough," said Michael. "But the mission we're considering is relatively limited. We will remotely access the private quarters of the Ruler and mentally map the space. This way, you can gain some credibility with him."

"Aren't there a ring of *Minders* around him?" asked Delphi.

Michael hid his surprise that Delphi knew this. "Leave it to me to help you gain access. If you're a natural, it shouldn't take more than three or four lessons."

"OK," said Delphi, wondering if it could be taught that easily. "One more thing. What is Tiffany's job besides helping me stay alive?"

"I'm afraid that information is compartmentalized. But I assure you she has other tasks and talents. You can share some minor matters with me, if you wish. I wouldn't worry too much about the details, though. Vance has thoroughly worked out the plans and has a good instinct for what will work."

"Alright," said Delphi. "I'm on board."

CHAPTER IX
REMOTE SURVEILLANCE

During a private moment with Delphi, Detinna remarked, "I heard Michael is training you."

"Oh, I see that Vance's compartmentalization only goes so far."

"So, what's it about?"

"Well, I suppose I can trust you. It's an out-of-body technique. I'm supposed to remotely access a highly secure space. I would think it would be too well guarded for relative amateurs like me."

"Maybe the Resistance is one step ahead in the psychic arms race. I've been wondering though. What if something happens to you? What if you don't come back after all this? I'm not talking about the remote viewing, but if and when you see the Ruler. Do you think he's going to let you go afterwards, if we fail?"

"I'm coming back one way or the other," said Delphi. "We've always come back to each other."

"Sometimes things don't work out."

"I suppose that's possible, but you'll be alright if I don't. There'll always be a Resistance, and they'll protect you. There are people like Michael who are grateful for what we did."

"That nerd? Give me a break. He may be younger, but that's all. And what if I don't make it back for some reason? You'd find somebody?"

"Nobody can replace you. After all, we've saved each other too much to consider anything else."

"Well, the first time, I left you behind."

"That's ancient history. The thing is that good has come out of all of this, and we've got more good to do. One day, we'll happily retire from all this drama and have a normal life again."

"Are you ready?" asked Michael.

"I'm still concerned about risks. Aren't there defenses against a dream body?" asked Delphi.

"Who said anything about using a dream body?"

"You don't mean we're going to go there in person?"

"No, the technique will be more like entering a person's mind."

"Isn't that impossible unless they're willing?" asked Delphi.

"There is a method that works, if the subject is in an altered state. Our subject generally does some drinking in the evening. Due to our sources, we'll know exactly when that occurs. Then, our actual intervention will be such that the subject won't even be aware."

"I suppose you'll be entering the mind of one of the household crew."

"No. We're thinking the Ruler himself. He won't suspect such an intrusion and will be overconfident in repelling it."

"Isn't he trained to do a reverse detection?"

"Yes, he's been trained in the defensive arts. But we have a new technique that is hard to pre-empt at first. You'll be gone before he knows it. And you're only looking at what he sees, not prying out specific information. You may, however, pick up his mind set and a stray thought or two which might prove useful."

"So, assuming we are able to see his inner sanctum by using our high-end psychic powers in order to suitably impress him, won't he more likely think that we've just accessed his housekeeper?"

"True, but it would be a breach, nonetheless.... He will more likely think it's due to his paramour. Maybe you can make a reference, if he goes that way, and create a degree of uncertainty and confusion. For the short term, he will have to consider that you're bona fide and wonder what else you know. More importantly, he will likely hear you out."

"And if not?"

"You'll be detained and there's another plan."

"One with a greater chance of success?"

"No. I think this plan is our best plan."

"And that's maybe 50%," Delphi mulled, wondering if there was anything more that Michael wasn't telling him. "I don't know if I like the odds."

Michael shrugged. "It's always tough odds to bring down an empire. We've done a lot just to come to this point. What's the alternative—wait for better odds that may never come?"

Delphi wanted more. His life and liberty were on the line. Detinna would ultimately be impacted. "What's the weak link in the plan?"

Michael paused a moment. "I'd say the Ruler himself. He's more resourceful than we've given credit and may sniff out our plan before we succeed."

"Then, we'll all be facing the gulag . . ."

"I think death would be better."

"One other thing. What's the Ruler's weakness?" asked Delphi.

"Aside from an attraction to young women—which is true for most men of power—I'd say that he underestimates the power of the occult."

"I'm visualizing the space," Delphi reported. "I can see it. It's like I can enter the photograph."

"Good, in fact remarkable," said Michael. "You're able to enter the mind of a hardened soldier, if only for a few seconds. You've seen the ritual space and a regional command center. We were rebuffed at the targeted location, primarily because we encountered an unexpected layer of security. I think the Ruler recently assigned new Minders in his quarters."

"Can you tell me a little more about the Minders?"

"Alert sensitives, who can block out-of-body intruders. They are highly skilled.

"So what are we going to do about them?"

"We need to create a diversion."

"And what if one of the Minders isn't diverted and sees us?"

"They would only see the Ruler and sense another force within him. It would be momentary, and I suppose they would be hesitant to challenge him. The Ruler will be defensive about having allowed someone entering his mind. If, for some reason, they do identify your intrusion, it could become a psychic battle. That's not a problem. I can handle a Minder or two."

"I have a feeling that things could spin out of control."

"Not really, other than being wrenched back here prematurely. A bad headache, a day or two in bed at most.... Things should work out."

"Alright," said Delphi, not convinced. "One more thing. Just in case. I think I should do a will. Who will take care of Detinna, if things don't work out?"

"Of course, our back up people would provide her a safe place. We've had good success at certain sites for non-detection, and probabilities remain good even if our immediate endeavor fails. But let's not think of failure. The odds have become much better now that you've joined us."

The room was suddenly illumined with red flashing lights. A call sounded to enter the central chamber. Everyone made their way in, and a ring of outer doors sealed.

"What is it?" asked Detinna.

"A precaution," Vance explained. "The surrounding area is being scanned by micro flying devices. Some just entered our immediate perimeter. They've finally gotten around to searching a straight line from our original flight path. We are lucky none of us were outside at the time."

The group waited an hour. "Still one in the area," Clare reported. "And they appear to be leaving isolates along the way."

"Expensive, but diligent," said Vance. "And it complicates our departure."

"We could inactivate any device on our path," suggested Clare. "It would sound a low level alert, but the devices do go out from time to time. It would take some time to check it out and we would be long gone."

"Hmm, inactivation can be tricky," mulled Vance. "And if we make a mistake, we're detected."

"At least we're clear from honing signatures," Clare remarked.

"What do you mean?" asked Delphi.

"A micro transmitter chip placed in persons," explained Tiffany. "Very difficult to detect unless they're activated. If one of us had one, we would have been detected by one of the micro-scanners that flew near here. It has to be close enough to activate the device and its signal."

"You mean one of us might have been implanted?" asked Detinna.

"They tend to implant persons who are considered possible risks. Often those held in detention."

"I've been in detention," said Delphi.

Detinna added, "And you said they did an operation to remove a cyst."

"Yes, they insisted on removing a benign tumor, one of the moles on my back."

Vance considered for a second, then said. "We need to leave now. Don't stop to get anything. This way."

Vance hit a switch, and a staircase in the center of the room opened. The group tumbled down fifteen feet and entered a chamber. A sealed door closed behind them as lights turned on. On a wall there were emergency packs, which Vance handed to each person.

Just as the last pack was handed out, there was a shudder above. "This way!" cried Vance.

He hit a button, and a door opened. The five ran into the corridor and the door automatically closed behind them.

Vance paused long enough to hit a switch. Another shudder sounded, then a thud. "They won't find much above," he said. "Probably destroyed a few robots and maybe an advance team as well, if they were quick enough. We still have a problem though. Delphi's hot."

"What do you think, Tiffany?" asked Vance "Can you get it out?"

"Should be able to, if I can find it. The mole was likely a diversion. There are three popular locations and two of them below the belt. But I think I can find it."

"We'll do it in the supply room before we exit," said Vance.

A half hour later, they reached a dead end and a panel.

"That was some tunnel," said Clare. "Even I didn't know about it."

Vance put in a coded transmission, which opened a hidden side door. Tiffany directed Delphi inside and opened a surgical kit.

The second try was a success. "Back side is easier than the front," she announced with a grin. "Sorry about the lack of anesthetic."

The party moved into the supply room. Delphi winced as he moved.

"You alright?" asked Detinna.

"I'll survive. It just won't be easy to sit for a while."

"Should we use the device as a decoy?" asked Tiffany, holding the speck-sized microchip with a pair of tweezers.

"Destroy it," said Vance. "It will take time for them to discover the tunnel and then the device's silence will make them think we're either dead or still underground."

Vance and Clare pulled out three long, folded gliders from behind a panel. "Simple to use. Two man gliders. Just hold on to the handles," Vance instructed.

They made their way back to the dead-end corridor, following Vance, who put his hand against the surface, then punched a pattern against the wall. A door to the outside opened. The group found themselves overlooking a gorge, with rushing water below. The height was breathtaking, and a cool wind rushed in.

"They won't think we're going this way," Tiffany observed.

Vance gave instructions. "We'll go in pairs, everyone with an experienced jumper. Clare and I. Michael and Detinna. Tiffany and Delphi. Aim for the far side of the gorge. Don't land in the river. There are rapids further down and a waterfall. Let's go."

The glide downwards was exhilarating. Delphi and Tiffany, the last to jump, were caught by a crosscurrent, blowing them further up river. Tiffany managed to stay on the right side of the river. The others were already specks.

Tiffany cursed, then said, "Didn't they consider wind currents crossing a gorge? They should have placed the opening nearer to a bend."

A few moments later they heard sudden popping sounds, then saw flashes of lights.

Tiffany's voice rang in alarm. "It's an ambush! They knew we were coming!"

Tiffany risked turning on her transmitter and caught Vance's faltering voice. "Hit bad, not going to make it ... the others captured. See you in Hawaii. Greece next."

Tiffany clicked off. "We're out of here. Hang on."

She turned left, riding the current to extend the flight as long as possible.

"I can't believe it," said Delphi. "Vance dying and everyone captured! Just like that? What happened?"

"They shouldn't have been there. They found out somehow."

"What's this about Hawaii and Greece?"

"Hawaii means flee to a safe zone and protect the principle. Greece is you."

"Me?"

"Yes. You're the new leader."

CHAPTER X
TW0 ANIMALS IN THE WILD

Delphi felt the ground under him shift in more ways than one. "What do you mean? I've just joined ... I've barely—"

"Don't think about it now. We've got to survive first. And we're likely to run into some action on the ground ahead."

Tiffany directed the glider along the tree line to the right of the river.

"What will happen to the others?"

"Hopefully not much, if we succeed with our plan. But we've got to make it through the next hour."

Tiffany directed the glider close to the river bank, then landed along on a stretch after a bend. Quickly, she bundled the glider and led Delphi under the cover of trees.

"Good, they're not here yet. We have a little time."

"But we're on foot. They're bound to catch us."

"Not if they think we're animals. Strip any metal off your clothes: belt buckle, zipper, and any devices. Take off your shirt, rub dirt on your body. We'll mimic the movement of deers."

"Will that fool them?"

"There're a lot of infrared signatures of animals, as this is a hunting area for some of the empire's elite. The animal's movements have to be patterned out, or there would be too many false positives. Don't try to flee from the point of capture. They'll find that pattern in an instant. We have to remain undetected for at least two days. Then we'll make our next move."

The facts slowly sunk into Detinna's mind. *Vance is dead. Delphi and Tiffany are missing, and the rest are captured.* She, along with the survivors, had been bound, hooded, gagged, and put in orange jumpsuits. A drug was administered that made her feel groggy and would soon put her out. They were airborne already, and she was barely able to sense anything except the low drone of the aircraft.

How could it have come to this? Detinna asked herself. She fought the grogginess by biting her lip. The rest of her body felt numb. *We had escaped close calls before.*

She thought she recognized a voice through an ear muff that wasn't fully on, as her hair was bunched under. "There's two left, a man and a woman—a natural and a survival expert," said the voice.

"Their area is cordoned off. They won't escape," said another.

"Find the man at all costs." The first voice she suddenly recognized. It was Michael's!

The betrayal caused Detinna to emit a moan as she drifted out of consciousness.

Detinna awoke in a white paneled cell filled with a steady white noise. The interrogators would be coming soon, no doubt. What could she tell them? If Michael was the plant, they would already know most everything regarding her contact with the Resistance. Why not simply tell the truth? If there was any chance of escaping, it lay in factors outside of her control. *What would Delphi be able to do without Vance? But Tiffany is with Delphi, a survival expert. They will be running together in the wild....*

Everything had been turned upside down. It seemed unlikely that the Resistance could succeed any time soon, and she would be in detention for an indeterminate period. She fought back tears. The reality of her separation from Delphi and an uncertain future seemed worse than the interrogation she would have to face.

Colonel Daniel had risen through the ranks, even though he started as a lowly border agent. He had a certain ruthless efficiency that left no stone upturned and produced results when others had failed. The Ruler brought him in specially for this mission. "Find them," he simply said. "Alive, if possible."

Daniel hated the ambiguity. It was easier to kill. But if it could be done, he would take them alive. There was no doubt in his mind that he would find them. In the wilderness there weren't other people to mix or blend with. There were caves and rock formations, but the runners would eventually surface to survive. He had checked on the Resistance woman. She was a survival and explosives expert, which caused concern. That might delay things. Still, it was only a matter of time.

Daniel went to the "theater" where several massive computer screens were displayed. The largest were in the central area, with others to the side showing various quadrants. "Shift to infra-red sensors. No human activity in a three-mile radius," reported the control agent.

"Turn on everything," said Daniel.

"It will show up any animal, even hedgehogs."

"Everything," repeated Daniel.

The infrared was dotted with movement. "OK, see if you can reduce it to objects over 40 kilograms."

The screen erased considerably, but there were still numerous dots, many in pairs.

"Kill all objects that are moving out of the cordoned sector," ordered Daniel. He would not want unnecessarily kill the targets, but he would rather have them dead than missing.

"That's a lot of ordinance. Don't you want to trace their movements for a while?"

"Do it," said Daniel.

The ground shook in the area as plumes went up from precision ordinance. "Keep moving, first away from the explosion, then drift to the right, " said Tiffany. "Keep to my side."

"We'll be moving closer to the kill zone."

"Animals don't know about kill zones. Now, change speeds. Run for fifty yards, then stop."

Delphi ran until he was out of breath. He laughed wildly. *All the technology of the modern state is bearing down on two mud-streaked persons. It's strangely exhilarating to be unencumbered and running for your life....*

An explosion sounded two hundred yards to their left. Then they glimpsed another low flying missile passing overhead. Tiffany realized the pattern. The explosions were along the perimeter of the cordon, keeping them within.

Tiffany signaled for Delphi to stop, then whispered. "Meander for a while, a little apart."

They moved closer within what Tiffany guessed was the center of the cordon, with a path angled partly angled away. Tiffany began to use only hand signals.

Delphi complied without questioning. He had begun to feel the bonding that goes with trusting another with your life. He knew they were going to have to work closely together to survive. He thought of Detinna. She had her fears, but he didn't doubt that he would remain faithful.

As light diminished, Tiffany and he stopped for a few minutes to rest. Then, to the point of tiredness, they wandered about a field as if foraging.

Night fell. Time to bed. Tiffany signaled, and she began collecting a nest of brush and leaves.

"What about me?" asked Delphi, breaking silence. "Should I collect--"

Tiffany spoke in a low voice. "The temperature drops at night, and we'll need to keep warm enough to sleep. And deer tend to sleep together.

Tiffany was all business. They lay down.

"Is it alright to talk?" asked Delphi after they had settled in.

"Whispers," said Tiffany.

"How did you get recruited? You seem like an unlikely person to be in this business."

"If you mean an unlikely person as being an attractive woman, you should know that all types are recruited. I can see we are going to have to get you up to speed some, if you're going to be the leader."

"Are you serious about that? I've just joined the Resistance. And if this isn't a joke, why me?"

"Vance had his reasons. He had the gift of seeing ahead. He must have thought that were going to need your talents for the final push."

"Won't that make me the most wanted person by the State?"

"I think you're already as wanted as much as can be. Perhaps being the official leader even gives you more leverage. They're less likely to kill you outright, for one."

"You never answered my question. Why did you join?"

"I suppose I can tell you, as you have all clearances now. My brother is a prisoner. I got in so I could help free him."

"Why don't you just try to spring him?"

"Not much chance from a secure facility. Very rarely do any escape, and you were one of them. I think it's actually easier to free him in the roundabout way, overthrowing the regime."

"But I still don't understand. Does your group really know about me?"

"We have a good-sized file on you. The State is not the only who keeps intelligence."

A sudden wave of exhaustion hit Delphi, and he closed his eyes. "One more thing. Not a word about our sleeping arrangements to my wife. She wouldn't understand."

"I know," said Tiffany. "Good night."

Delphi's dreams were disturbing. He was fleeing from fiery darts. One fell out of the sky, struck his back and caused an intense flash of pain.

Delphi told the dream when he woke.

"I'm afraid your dream is a realistic fear. There are drones that shoot at moving objects without clearance. They've probably lowered the threshold for firing. We'll have to keep an eye out for them."

In a cell lit only by a monitor and a light on Detinna's face, there was a tense pause.

"It's hard to believe," said the interrogator. "Yet, your read-outs are consistent."

"I have nothing to hide," said Detinna. "There's a lot I don't know. They compartmentalize stuff I wasn't in on."

"The only thing is Delphi's mission."

"Yes, we've been over that. They were planning to remotely access the Ruler's chambers."

"How would that be possible? They must know that we have considerable counter measures."

"I don't know. I wasn't in on the details."

"He didn't reveal any techniques?"

"They hadn't trained him yet, much less me."

"This woman Tiffany. What do you know about her?"

"Expert in explosives and survival." Detinna fought to keep her emotion neutral, for she did not want to reveal any weakness that could be used against her.

"She wasn't training him?" The interrogator expected there to be some jealousy.

"No, Michael was."

"Did Delphi feel he was competent?"

"I don't know . . . I – "

The interrogator noted that the reading altered.

"I suppose . . . I've been wondering if there was a plant, as we were found. It had to be someone . . . I didn't know anyone's background—this Tiffany . . ."

"You seem irritated at her."

"Maybe she was the plant," offered Detinna, putting forth her first untruth. The readings didn't pick up an anomaly, for her intense feelings overrode them.

"Was there a reason to suspect her?"

"She had looks and could use them to get information. She was highly trained. I don't know. I'm not a spy master. As you know, we were dragged into this."

The interrogator felt something was missing. There always was, but the read-outs were within the expected range. The woman had told him near everything. There was nothing much more here, in all likelihood, and she was probably no direct threat. But a preventive detention would surely be deemed necessary for anyone this close to a principle. More importantly, she could serve as a lure. He felt unease that a person, who seemed to be just caught up in a thing, could be detained indefinitely, and decided to do something for her. He wrote in his report: "Cooperative, likely to remain cooperative if normal comforts are provided."

Evasion was exhausting––the constant weaving back and forth, the sudden spurts, and the periods of non-movement. The pace was more demanding when they traveled over exposed areas and when was no cloud cover. Delphi had to keep his attention focused, imitating Tiffany. He felt he was becoming a mirror to her, then he felt a sudden stab, remembering Detinna. Where was she? Were they interrogating her or something worse? What would he do if she were indefinitely detained?

The two had just moved into an open field when Delphi heard whirring and saw a puff of dirt to his side. He turned, heard a second whirring, then felt a sudden stab to his left shoulder. Delphi fell down, stunned, more from being unexpectedly struck.

Tiffany helped him up immediately. "Keep moving," she said. "Your muscles will tighten otherwise. Follow me."

Delphi struggled to obey despite the pain that radiating down his arm and into his back. He heard more whirring sounds, then saw more poofs. More darts striking the earth.

The pair crossed the field and into tree cover when Delphi fell over, exhausted. Tiffany inspected him.

"What is it?"

"A dart from a small drone. They must be shooting at all moving objects within a size range. They're trying to sort the animals from the human. A deer your size would only be a little slowed by one of these."

"I'm feeling numb in my left arm."

"Let me check again." Tiffany did more than look as Delphi winced. She pulled out an arrow like object with saw-like edges.

"Primitive, but effective. Good thing it wasn't a more advanced model."

"Even if it they're old models, I vote we stay out of their path."

"I'm doing my best to avoid them," said Tiffany, helping Delphi up. "Keep close. We'll go as one animal now."

"I'm sorry," said Delphi, who put considerable weight on her.

"First rule. Survival of the leader."

"The numbing doesn't seem to be going away," said Delphi, after they had walked for thirty minutes.

"The toxin was programed to slow the subject for a retrieval. You should feel completely well tomorrow."

"But my back – the pain…. I don't know if I can go much further."

"Just a few more minutes, and we'll stop for the day."

"Won't we be breaking the pattern?"

"It's a risk we'll have to take. Hopefully, we won't be triggered for visual surveillance. Up ahead, there's deeper forest and rocks."

Colonel Daniel studied the read-outs. How could they still be missing? He had expanded the perimeter to include the furthest extent a glider could reach, plus an extra 5 miles, but had turned up a blank. The woman was a survival expert, but that should only have delayed capture.

He considered that they might have died and been swept down river. But no bodies had been found. He started to list other possibilities. They had returned to the center and were hiding out. Yet this area was the most extensively searched. If they were hiding, they would soon have to come out for food and water. They couldn't have carried but the bare minimum of supplies if they were gliding. Another possibility was that they had a back-up craft hidden. But the satellite coverage had turned up negative.

Daniel directed the full screen to show all living forms. There were too many animals. He had wanted simply to kill all the larger sized ones within the circle, but the Ruler would not tolerate a general slaughter of his preserve. They had settled on stunning all objects showing a general movement away from the center.

Daniel reviewed the data regarding outgoing craft and concluded the two were still there. He decided to send out a fleet of the latest model drone stunners to sweep the area, whether they were coming or going or laying still. The stunners would be set at a moderate toxin level that should immobilize the target for 12 hours—enough for teams to visually inspect the bodies. Almost all animals would likely survive. Some would die, but Daniel would rather risk the Ruler's wrath at that, than an escape by leaders of the Resistance.

"Do more than you think is necessary when nothing turns up," was a dictum he followed. He had to be sure. The Ruler was not known for his patience. Daniel gave the orders.

CHAPTER XI
BURIED

Detinna noticed improvements after the questioning stopped. She had better food, two exercise periods, a daily shower, and access to approved books. It was disheartening just the same. She was isolated except for contact with her jailers. She feared she had been deemed not to have any more vital information and would be forgotten. Unless the Resistance succeeded, she would grow old here. She knew too much. Michael had betrayed them.

Detinna couldn't stop the flow of questions that streamed into her head. Was Delphi still alive, or had he been captured? Wouldn't it have been better to have been captured before all this contact with the Resistance? Hadn't their flight from home worked against them? Was there any chance that she would be released?

Detinna realized she had to come up with a plan that would give her hope. Slowly, she formed one in her mind.

"They're coming," said Tiffany.

"I don't see anything."

"I sense it. We've been in the area too long. They're bound to run a complete sweep before they move on."

"A complete sweep?"

"That will kill every living animal over a certain size within the perimeter."

"I guess that includes us. What do we do?"

"Dig. We start digging."

Tiffany studied the landscape, then followed an outcrop of rocks. There were no overhangs or caves, just varied shapes of gray stone jutting out of the earth. She paused before one shaped like a bowl, smoothed by the ocean of million years ago. An occasional ancient coral could be seen encrusted.

"This is as good as we'll get," she said.

Tiffany broke a stone to make a sharp edge. Then, with several controlled hits on a tree branch, she formed a rough digging tool. "Go as deep as you can," she said, handing the tool to Delphi. "Build up an earth mound on the exposed side. I'll be back."

Delphi felt a wave of anxiety. "Do you think it's a good idea to separate?"

"This won't take long," she said, taking a large flake from the broken stone with her.

A few minutes later, Tiffany returned with an armful of leafy saplings to make a roof over the hollow.

Delphi had only been able to dig a foot and a half before the ground became hard and rocky. It took another hour of the two alternating to make a hollow large enough for them both.

"Won't they read our signatures through the brush?" asked Delphi.

"We'll cover the bower with dirt. It will be messy, but earth is the best heat absorber."

They had half covered the bower when the air became filled with a buzzing sound. A shot sliced into a nearby tree trunk, and a glistening metal disc dripped with toxins. The two remained motionless.

"We've been spotted?" said Delphi.

"No. We would have been hit if we had been spotted. Most likely they're shot-gunning the place to flush out any prey."

A few moments later they heard a terrifying howl from an animal.

"Quickly, cover the rest. The hard part follows," said Tiffany. "We'll have to wait them out until new animal movement comes through."

"How long?"

"At least 12, maybe 24 hours before we sight undrugged animals."

"A day in here?"

"A day of survival. At least you can recuperate. We'll have another problem when we emerge. We'll have to find a couple of replacements."

"Replacements?"

"We have to find two animals to kill so we can become their signature."

"How are we going to kill them?"

"Leave that to me."

Delphi lay down, and only then did he realize how exhausted he was. It wouldn't take long before he was asleep.

"Have you considered giving ourselves up?" asked Delphi, wondering if they would make it out alive. "And what are our chances out here?"

"Giving up is not an option. Admittedly, whoever's in charge out there is thorough. But they don't have any leads yet as to our exact location. He probably thinks that we've already left, so he's just covering all bases. Then he'll refocus the search. If that happens, we should make it out."

"Alright," said Delphi. "Time to sleep."

Delphi slept soundly into the next day.

"An animal's coming," said Tiffany, waking Delphi mid-morning.

Delphi was awake but left his eyes closed after opening them briefly. He was still dead tired. The intimacy of the rock cocoon seemed to be too much at first, but the occasional whirring of drones and his flashbacks of pain overrode that concern. It reminded Delphi of his childhood, hiding in the woods.

"There," whispered Tiffany. Delphi opened his eyes and watched as Tiffany emerged. A deer with a red scar that grazed its side was slowly walking by them.

Tiffany waited with a sharpened stone and stick. The deer, still groggy from toxin, didn't seem to notice her approach. She came close enough to strike the beast, then both stopped and stood still for several moments

What is she waiting for? Delphi wondered.

Tiffany slowly reached out and stroked the beast, focusing on the side of its head. Then she put her belt around the beast's neck and called out to Delphi, "This is our ticket out."

Nothing has turned up, Daniel kept repeating in his mind. All the animals in the human weight class had been stunned. They had all been located, photographed and tagged to be eliminated from the computer. Still, there was a possibility that they had been missed.

The question remained for him as to what more to do. Should he consider the search of the immediate area done and devote his resources to a much wider, dispersed area?

He felt a trace of unease. Something had been missed. They should not have gone undetected this long. Daniel felt a grudging respect. If he captured the survival expert alive, he would consider trying to turn her to his side.

For now, he had a decision to make. The Ruler had been upset at the deaths of two bears. Daniel passed it off to old programs with some of the drones. But the Ruler would not tolerate any more deaths.

While he was debating what to do, he got a rare operational order from the Ruler. "Sweep the area manually, quadrant by quadrant."

Was that really necessary? Daniel wondered. The search could take days and be exorbitant in resources, especially if the two had already escaped the net. He had little choice but to obey the Ruler's whim.

It was the last step and better than robotic means. He ordered one hundred two-person teams to sweep the area and shoot on sight. If the survival expert was as good as she had been thus far, it would cost too much to take her alive.

Tiffany and Delphi walked with the deer, which Tiffany was constantly soothing with her right hand. Her left still held the weapon.

"Won't the deer bolt when the toxin wears off?" asked Delphi

"I'm afraid we'll have to kill it before that. We can't have one signature become two."

They trudged for miles until they were weary. When the deer finally lay down, they rested next to it.

"Have you ever thought that life would be a lot easier if we just went along with things?" asked Delphi.

"Easier for the short term," Tiffany half agreed. "At what point do you risk realizing that you've saved your life, only to have not really lived? When my life is nearly done, I don't want to have such regrets. After the United Federation did away with the Senate and the Judiciary, checks on the executive ceased, and things got really intolerable. So much inequality, arbitrary treatment that the average person became radicalized and silent."

"Yes, but the general population hasn't joined the Resistance."

"Not officially. It's too risky for anyone to say or do anything. After a while you notice that the ones who speak out don't get anywhere or lose their jobs. Sometimes there are more drastic measures, but who can prove it? As for the majority of people, they're struggling to survive in jobs which demand more and more and force people to be focused on the small stuff. Some, like you, got caught up by circumstances because they ventured out of the box."

"But where did that get me? I'm wandering half naked with the animals and my wife is imprisoned."

"We will do our best to make sure she returns unscathed."

"How can you do anything? It's near impossible to escape. It will be easier to overthrow the empire."

"That's what we're planning to do," Tiffany replied.

Detinna obsessed about escape, although she knew it was impossible. At least five levels of security stood between her and the outside. She couldn't allow herself to grow old here. Somehow, she would have to find a way out.

She thought back to how it had all started. There was the encounter with Delphi in the other world, their narrow escape from the Time Thief, and then the Guatemalan trip, where Delphi almost lost his life. They were not crimes, but they broke unwritten rules about going beyond normal boundaries. It seemed the interrogator had sympathized with her and had gone easy on her. But, better conditions or not, they would still imprison her indefinitely.

It was almost worse than life imprisonment. With life, you knew what you were dealing with. With indefinite confinement, you were left the possibility that freedom could come any day. Then, as each day passed, the hope that it brought would slowly die. Freedom would only come––if death didn't count as such––with the fall of the empire. But how likely was that? The Resistance seemed like a long shot now.

Detinna's cell had no windows. Three slats of light filtered through a small air duct above. Occasionally she heard the faint sound of a bird cheep, a reminder of an outside world. She tried to visualize Delphi, but came up blank. She didn't even know if he was dead or alive.

Her only recourse, it seemed, was to cooperate as much as possible and make the best of a bad situation. There was also one more thing she could do. She would ask to see the warden.

Tiffany sensed something. Maybe it was quieter than usual. Maybe there was a sound out of place.

"We need to hide," she said.

"What's happening?"

"A ground patrol is near. I didn't expect a physical search. If that's the case, we're likely to get caught with the deer or not."

"There's not much cover here. "

"The cover is up in the trees," said Tiffany. "Let's hope they don't train their scanners up regularly."

Tiffany selected a tree with thick limbs and foliage about a dozen feet up. "We'll let the deer go free here. Hopefully it will distract them."

They had just settled into position when Tiffany spotted motion. "They're coming," she said, helping to position Delphi up. "Stay behind the trunk and remain motionless. Take this," she added, handing the digging stick to Delphi. "You may need to use it."

"Just like the cave days," muttered Delphi.

They waited, and Delphi felt something sliding along his neck.

"Great, there're ants."

"Silence."

It seemed a long time and that the patrol might pass when they heard voices close by. "He's persistent, give him that," said the voice. "He's bringing in second teams to cover the same ground. Keeping us on our toes."

"What's the scanner say?"

"Nothing."

"You don't even have it on!"

"They're long gone by now. We're only two miles from the down point, and they've been missing for three days. They're probably in some cave by the border by now."

"Then we've got it easy. Go ahead, turn it on."

"Well, there's a faint reading … nothing. Perhaps a deer was there."

"That wouldn't set it off. Another false reading. What is it this time? A dead animal? An underground anomaly? Sometimes when you turn them on, they just buzz off."

"Should I bring in a sweep team?"

"Sweeping leaves? We don't want to look like fools. We'll check it out ourselves."

They stepped under the tree.

One of the men started relieving himself.

"Hey that messes up the signature."

"Gotta go. You and I both know——"

Tiffany suddenly dropped from the ground and with a swing of her legs tripped the man relieving himself. She cried out to Delphi, then dove her head into the gut of the second man as he reached for his gun. The man blanched and his weapon was secured by Tiffany.

By this time Delphi dropped with staff in hand and hit the first man on the head.

Then Tiffany fired two quick energy bursts, killing both.

Delphi was aghast. "Did you have to do that?"

"We need two signatures. I didn't have time to change the settings they had their guns on. Dress up now."

"They'll find out. They have communication equipment."

"It will be mostly static on the receiving end."

"How much time till they discover we're not them?"

"Depends what type of controls they've put in place. But it's going to be nip and tuck for a while."

CHAPTER XII
CLEAN SWEEP

Detinna had tried to make herself as attractive as possible. She had no makeup, just soap for cleaning. Since her new privileges, she had been given one set of street clothes and she wore these. Unless help came from the outside, it was her only remaining card, her attractiveness and her powerlessness.

Her request to the warden was granted. No doubt he had these requests before. No doubt such a meeting would be considered potentially useful and part of the interrogation.

When Detinna stepped in the door, she saw that the warden immediately considered whether she was looking for an exchange. Detinna gave him credit, however. He remained professional and courteous. The middle-aged man, who wore an impeccable gray suit, directed her to sit and waited for her to speak. Detinna couldn't bring herself to say anything and a silence hung in the air.

The warden didn't appear to be bothered. "I've been reading your file," he finally said. "By all accounts, it looks like you got caught up in something beyond your control. Even your husband probably never intended to be part of the Resistance."

"We didn't," said Detinna, weakly. "Can anything be done?"

The warden smiled, but it was not from taking pleasure at her situation.

"You must know that I have little freedom to direct this matter. Perhaps after your husband is captured, an arrangement can be made."

"Is there something...?" said Detinna, unable to finish the sentence.

"I will do the best to make your stay here comfortable."

Detinna felt her chance to somehow alter things had passed. "I feel so alone," she managed to say.

"I can do one more thing," added the warden. " You can be granted access to an entertainment room."

"Thank you," said Detinna, realizing she had failed. She would not plead or beg. She had asked once.

Detinna lingered a moment, waiting for the guards. The man looked up at her. There was a moment when their eyes met and something was communicated.

"I would like to see you next week, so you can tell me how you like the entertainment," said the warden.

Colonel Daniel examined the read-outs from both human and automated teams. The sweep was thorough and the effort intensive. He was even questioned by the high command about applying so much attention to the immediate radius when his targets were now likely outside the perimeter. He had responded with one of his dictums often proved true: *proximity was the most likely possibility.*

Daniel surveyed the many blips on the screen, some moving, some still. He noticed two blips on the screen—a search detail—had remained stationary for over thirty minutes. They had been walking for three hours prior since early morning and probably were tired, even bored. Still, a thirty minute break was excessive. "Check Sector 204," he radioed. "Tell them we want to wrap this up by day's end."

Daniel wondered about his next step. The intelligence he received from the interrogation unit had been minimal. The woman had told all she knew. She even revealed the name of the Being, confirmed by her diary. The Ruler had thought that might come in useful. The warden had transferred the captive off the interrogation unit. He wondered if this was intentional favoritism. In the end she might turn out to be their best bait to draw her husband out.

Daniel knew that the Ruler's patience was limited. *She is the possible key to a quick resolution,* he thought. *We could release her.* It would take some selling to the Ruler. The warden shouldn't be a problem, for he was known as being soft on women, particularly if they were innocent. Right now, however, he had to make sure that obvious things were done.

"Have you checked Sector 204?" he radioed back.

"Just getting to it."

"What's delaying you?"

"We had a friendly fire incident in 528. A man is down."

"Alright, I'll handle it," said Daniel. "Patch me in."

The line opened. "Commander Daniel to Sector 204. Report in"

There was no immediate answer. Daniel repeated the request.

There was static on the line, then a faint gruff voice. "Sector clear. We're moving slowly. Ankle badly sprained."

"Do you need a medic?"

"No. We'll be alright, just slower."

Daniel signed off. Things happen in the field, a man down, a team member injured.

For a moment something alarmed him. They hadn't offered a pass code, but neither did he ask for it, which was protocol. They were probably surprised that the search leader had called them. It was a lapse in protocol. He thought of calling back to verify, but he did not want to call attention to his mistake.

"Something's going on in sector 205," he heard a voice say. "A fire of unknown origin." It was one of the many people watching monitors.

Danielle glanced at the map. By coincidence it was near to Sector 204. Or was it?

"Check it out with a Special Team."

He took a last look at Sector 204. The two searchers were moving on, one blip slower than the other. He put a tracer on their pattern to see if anything more unusual happened. Daniel called to mind another of his dictums: Single anomalies occur, a second occurs on occasion, a third is a pattern.

Delphi's eyes widened when the call came in. They were burying the bodies. Tiffany had almost responded too late.

"We're not fully in the clear," she said, after the bodies were covered. "That was Daniel, leader of the search. It almost made me think that he knew who we were and was toying with us. He missed us—a rarity. My guess is that it won't be long before he realizes his mistake. We need to move fast."

"Isn't one of us supposed to have a sprained ankle?"

"We need to cross over into the neighboring quadrants. There's not much time."

"I hate to ask what the odds are now. They'll eventually find these bodies."

"For the immediate future, our odds have gone up. We are disguised, and we have weapons. We can also listen in on communications."

Delphi felt dazed. "I guess it's finally sunk in. I'm fully in now."

"I'm afraid you reached that point some time ago."

Tiffany led Delphi along a stream overarched with branches when they spotted another team.

"Don't get yourself killed by moving too fast," they heard the communicator say.

Tiffany responded as if to a threat. "Identify yourself."

The other team responded with the code word, "Fireball."

"OK, we're just trying to get home quicker. See anything?"

"Just some charred deer."

Tiffany clicked off and sighed.

"We're lucky," said Tiffany. "They gave us the pass code and they're entering our old sector. That should buy us more time."

Colonel Daniel was surveying the theater screens for the last time before he slept. The search was nearly complete, and so far, they had come up with nothing. He checked the tracker on the team in Sector 204 and saw that they had moved a fair distance. Was that likely if they had injury? They had, for some reason, crossed the path of another team, a breach in protocol. Suddenly, he realized he had his third anomaly, and he cursed under his breath. Neither team must be allowed to get away.

Daniel called to the current team in sector 204, and they responded with the proper codes. The voice didn't sound the same. In the neighboring quadrants, there were two other teams, and he ordered an assistant to quickly check the pass codes. He waited a few moments, and they both cleared. Had he been mistaken? He couldn't take that chance, he decided. They must be killed and checked post-mortem. It was unfortunate and would have to be explained. There was always friendly fire. It would be less consequence than if the targets got away.

Daniel gave the orders. The ground commander protested, but Daniel overrode his objection. "We're in Ultra threat status. Clean sweep starting with Sector 204, then move to the two adjoining sectors."

CHAPTER XIII
FREED

"You can call me Edward," said the warden.

Detinna wondered if she felt a little too comfortable. It seemed there would be no untoward demands. The access to the entertainment had helped her to deal with her solitude. Her conversation was still limited to a few words with her jailers when food was dropped off and as she was shown to the showers. She realized her vulnerability. Detinna felt the intense desire to be with someone. Wouldn't he be tempted to use that need at some point?

"I was wondering if you could tell me first-hand about your out-of-body experiences," asked Edward after some small talk. "The topic has always fascinated me. I read your report where you aided a novice in accessing highly guarded facilities. There was also the time you and your partner went to Guatemala and freed the Time Thief. I found it all quite interesting."

So it was to be a gentle, off-record interrogation. Detinna could either go along or refuse. But she had already told almost all the truth about things. Possibly, the warden had an actual interest in the topic. He seemed to be attentive to her as well. He might not refuse an advance, but neither would he proffer one. For now, she just talked. She had to be careful not to tell anything that might compromise Delphi.

"We're cooked," said Tiffany after the orders came over the air. "He's being too thorough. We need to start asking ourselves: do we allow ourselves to be captured or end it here? I think you should be taken alive, for it will distract them and help the cause. For my part, it's over. I couldn't stand to be imprisoned indefinitely."

"There must be another way," said Delphi with a sudden vehemence. For Tiffany, who had been risking her life for him––it was too much for him to give up.

A cracking sound sent their heads lower. Another team was crossing the path. Tiffany observed them carefully for a few moments, then said, "It's our lucky day. Set your guns to stun. We've got to take them out within the next thirty seconds. Just do as I say."

Delphi wondered why the sudden change of plans, but did as ordered.

"Point your gun to the ground by this rock."

Tiffany called out. "We've got them! Back up is needed!" She shouted the code for the transmitter. The other team rushed forward, a tall man and an equally tall woman.

The team reached Delphi and looked toward the empty ground. With two short bursts, Tiffany stunned them. "Bind them and wave down the next cruiser."

The Captain of the cruiser held a distaste for the job. Wiping out perfectly good teams was unheard of except in the most dire situation. He had eliminated one already. What was the emergency? So when the Captain got a call that a team had been captured, he ordered his ship and a support vehicle down. The jets reversed thrusters and settled as a helicopter. The two captives were bound and gagged.

"Good job," he said, although the team had not followed orders. The captives should have been killed immediately. But there was an attractive woman involved. The Captain ordered his men to escort the two prisoners aboard his ship, while the other team boarded the support vehicle.

"Don't forget to check in your weapons. Standard precaution," said the Captain.

After a moment's hesitation, Tiffany and Delphi gave up their weapons and boarded.

Daniel entered the interrogation room with expectation and a vague, unsettled feeling. He had ordered the teams killed, yet one was captive. He had heard that the officer, a transfer from an independent unit, had even been overhead, telling headquarters to do their own dirty work. He would deal with reprimands later, but he might gain some useful intelligence before the execution.

Through a one-way mirror, he viewed the bound team and saw terror in their faces. Something was missing. The survival person, the woman, did not appear to be assessing her possibilities for escape. Although it was obvious that she had little or no chance, her training required her to always be planning. Something was wrong.

Daniel ordered the prisoners ungagged, and they started talking in confused sentences. "They got away ... a man, a woman—aboard the cruiser."

Daniel didn't need any complicated machines to know they were telling the truth. He turned to his second officer. "A mistake has been made. Find the second cruiser and destroy it."

There was only a moment of hesitation before the order was conveyed, "What about these two?"

"You know the orders. It should have been done earlier."

Daniel hurried on to the situation room. He prided himself that he would not waste more time than necessary with the captives. He quickly found out that the suspect cruiser had already left, mixing with the fleet. It was not unexpected that they had overpowered the crew.

The ship had a unique transponder, but it had been turned off or altered. There were hundreds of ships in the immediate area, and more than one would be out of order. A few new ones might have signatures on the books, and there might be errors . . . Should he take out all the malfunctioning ones? Too many, he decided. Instead, Daniel ordered the space controllers to track all ships with an anomaly and attempt to identify the right one. It should still be a matter of time before they were caught.

Still, Colonel Daniel harbored uncertainty. The survival expert seemed to be guessing his moves, and while he followed their trail, they were always a step ahead. He needed to think two steps ahead.

In time their ship would need fuel. Daniel ordered all fueling stations to be placed on high alert, and at any hint of a discrepancy, to conduct a full security check. The question is where would they try to go next. He calculated the amount of fuel left and the radius. The search perimeter was expanded.

For the first time, the colonel wondered if he would fail. Usually, suspects with whom he had a hot lead were caught within 24 hours. He had the full resources of the state. He sensed that the Ruler's impatience would be growing.

As if on cue, a call came in from Central. Daniel steeled himself and turned on the video screen.

The Ruler had no time for pleasantries. "Are they captured?"

"No," was his simple reply.

No excuses were offered, although it seemed the Ruler waited for one. It disarmed him for a moment. "Sometimes I think they have a sixth sense.... What about the woman in detention?"

"The warden is working the soft approach," said Daniel. "It doesn't look like she has much to offer. Maybe we can turn her to our side over the long term. But I'm considering using her as a lure."

"Do what you have to do." After that the Ruler digressed. "This rag-tag group shouldn't be a threat. They've had luck on their side so far. I've considered replacing you, but you've taken out their leader, and you've served me well before. You have three days."

Daniel thanked the Ruler and considered his chances. If the two runners ditched their vehicle and laid low, he might not succeed. Such searches could take up to a week.

What would happen to him? Would he be demoted to some desk job at a remote location? Or worse? Daniel decided that he must take more drastic action to flush them out.

The detained woman was his insurance. She would be released and watched. There was a risk that things could mess up on the outside, but he couldn't afford to wait for events to fall his way.

Daniel got on the communicator and gave the order. "Free Detainee 697 and place a watch on her."

"What?" asked the warden.

"Can I make it any plainer? Free her immediately."

Within the hour, Detinna was walking free and carrying a full pass to access transportation. She could hardly believe it. Everything was the same, but everything was different. She didn't know how much time she had until things changed again. She was being watched, no doubt, although she saw no sign of it.

It didn't take long to gather why she had been freed. Delphi must have eluded them, and they hoped that he would try to see her again. He shouldn't put himself at risk, but his chances of retrieving her, no matter how well they tailed her, were far better than if she remained in maximum security.

There was no need for Detinna to go back to work. She had savings that she found had remained untouched. There would be no more time or focus for work, ever again, she thought. In fact, nothing would ever be normal again.

Detinna started to tour different parts of the city, preparing for the eventuality that Delphi would try to contact her. She had bought new clothes on the possibility that all her clothes had tracers. But what of her body? She spent some time searching her body for any trace of an incision, but had found none.

In a day of wandering, Detinna saw no sign of being followed, but she knew it was probable that a dedicated drone too small to be seen was doing the work. No word came from Delphi yet, but she remained alert.

"They must be desperate," said Tiffany. "She's been freed." Hidden in a cruiser in a vast parking lot, Tiffany had risked a communication with an inside source.

"What?" asked Delphi. "Who's been freed?"

"Detinna."

"Thank God," said Delphi, rising to leave.

"No, we've got to think this through. No doubt they have freed her to get to you. Of course, we want to help her out and bring her in with us. We have a far better chance of freeing her from unseen jailers. But we have to be careful. We must first get a message to her somehow and arrange a rendezvous. We should also give her a choice."

"A choice?" asked Delphi.

"If she comes to us, she will be actively choosing to join the Resistance. It seems that they mainly want you. Do you want to take a risk that both of you will be captured?"

"But if the ploy doesn't draw us out, won't they one day take her back in again?"

"Possibly, but she's free now...."

"And won't it be risky having her join us? Won't they have planted her with an embed?"

"I don't think so. There not be enough time for it to heal and it would be too obvious. It would keep her from trying to contact you. Maybe they gave her something in her food, which would only stay in her system for so long."

"What do we do next?" asked Delphi.

"We'll get a message to her. The one thing we have going for us is that they want to us to reach her. They'll allow some slack before they tighten the net. But if we're smart, we might just slip through.

"We'll need a plan to extract her, but we're ahead of ourselves," said Tiffany. "First, we have to ditch this vehicle. We need to reach a safe house. Each cell is atomized, but someone as high up as Michael might have had access to more than one location."

"Maybe a more distant house, one unlikely to be compromised."

"Fuel," said Tiffany. "We're too low, and all terminals are being watched. Let me think."

A moment later, Tiffany responded. "We'll have to do some old-fashioned stealing. We'll take a car with more fuel, then locate a safe house that's a standby that a higher up wouldn't likely know about. We won't tell anyone on our side and break into the house."

" I thought it was impossible to steal a cruiser these days."

"There are weaknesses in certain models and there's a sea of them out here. And I'm a pretty good thief."

Minutes later, they were gliding effortlessly in a luxurious aircar.

"Wow!" exclaimed Delphi. "I thought it would be harder to steal one of this class."

"There are emergency over-rides in advanced models. Usually, only police usually know, so they can commandeer a vehicle."

"It's great to sit back and relax. We could even spend the night here."

"Don't get too relaxed. This model only works for four hours before further verification is needed. And since we have none, the vehicle must be destroyed before then."

The Ruler felt uneasiness despite good news. The Resistance was in disarray. A sizeable number had been killed, captured, or were on the run. A major plot had been foiled. There were a few loose ends, which included the whereabouts of a few in the inner circle.

The Ruler looked down at the aging spots on his hands. They had become more prominent over the past few months. The last of his stolen years were ebbing away. Unless something was done soon, he would become irretrievably old. He needed a good source, and he needed one soon. The Ruler believed there was hope. His own specialist assured him he could deliver a subject to extend his renewal. There were also plans to capture the one who had undone the work of the Time Thief. Maybe he would know why the Ruler's years had been returned at only a fraction of the others.

The Ruler considered that his time could finally be coming to an end. If he had lived a hard life, and he might have been willing to let go. But he had been given too much. With his power, almost all of his wishes could be fulfilled and his pleasures met.

The Ruler gazed into a mirror. It was not what he expected to see. It was not how he felt. For a moment, he imagined letting go of his power, to disappear and become an unknown, and to not have to deal with threats of assassination and overthrow. He would just grow old and die like everyone else. He had enough power to accomplish his own disappearance.

The Ruler had begun to feel his body unable to renew a few years ago. From his three DNA clone bodies, almost all of his internal organs had been replaced at least once. He was due for a skin replacement and its signs of aging would go away once again. Still, he felt that something else was fundamentally altering. His brain was aging. He was forgetting things and losing capacity. There was no way, as yet, to transplant a brain. Experiments with transplanted neurons had given hope, but the implanted tissue often became invasive and the subject died. The Ruler shuddered. Maybe they would perfect the technique, but his chief scientists admitted it was decades away. His time was finally running out, unless....

There was another way. He could contact the Being who had once directed the Time Thief. The woman and the man had met the Being and had somehow been able to constrain it. He sensed the Being was the key. It was risky, but what choice did he have?

The Ruler had come to a decision. He was not yet ready to die. He reached Daniel and ordered, "Bring the woman to me."

Daniel was surprised by the sudden change in command. What was the Ruler hoping to accomplish by this? His plan had a good chance of flushing out the principle. Surely, the husband would attempt to communicate with the woman and bring her over to him. Now, it became much less likely that he would find Delphi in time.

Daniel had never disobeyed an order from the Ruler before, but this was about survival. He would have to delay him, somehow. Daniel decided to say that a contact was in process. "She's already on the way to meet the principle. You can have both if you wait."

"Very well," said the Ruler. "Give me a report first thing in the morning."

The Being was starved. It hadn't had a new victim since the Time Thief had dissolved and gone to a world beyond its control. Now it must find new food on its own. Although the Being had several prospects, none were ready. It usually found that those with power at high levels were more likely to succumb. It was natural for them to think that they could exceed limits and that there wouldn't be a price. The work was easier, although still difficult. Not many would give themselves for a benefit, no matter how great, for they knew it would one day end. They could have a few more years, maybe dozens.... More of their whims could be fulfilled, but it would never be enough, and it would end all too soon. There was too the underlying worry about the final result, just beyond their consciousness———for the dark nature of the Being could never be fully disguised by light.

The one called the Ruler was almost ready. He was under stress of maintaining his power and his own aging. *Had he exaggerated the powers of the couple who had gotten the Time Thief to accept death.* The Being itself was still bothered by that deed, but it would have to wait to address that matter. For now, it must feed itself and turn the Ruler its way. It would promise him enough years that he couldn't turn down. The Ruler would seal the deal by offering him a willing victim.

CHAPTER XIV
BARGAINS

The matter was still difficult—to find a *willing* victim. To accelerate things the Being would help bring a victim to the Ruler. There was a witch who had done its bidding in the past. She had a young female apprentice, her daughter. It sensed that she would offer her if the conditions were right. The Being summoned to itself a pleasant form, changed into a handsome man, and appeared on earth.

The communication came in suddenly. "Delphi, I'm nearby. Can we meet?"

It was Detinna. Delphi had already opened his mouth when Tiffany wrenched the communicator from his hand. "No Delphi here. Redirect."

The voice acknowledged and signed off.

Tiffany replied to Delphi's puzzle face, "The words were spliced together by a computer with changes in intonation to make it sound natural. They're running it on all frequencies. Anyone who responds will be stopped."

"Sorry, that was stupid, but we do we do?"

"Obviously, we need a plan for her to evade her Watchers. It won't be easy. My guess it that Detinna will be out and about, trying to give us a signal."

"We've had luck before, with trying the obvious. Why not try getting a message to her right at home?"

Tiffany considered, "She'll be too well covered. But that gives me an idea. Who lives on either side of you?"

"There's an elderly couple on one side and a young married couple on the other."

"Does the younger couple both work?"

"Yes."

"Good. I could pose as the woman. From there I might be able to establish contact, maybe from the backyard. Does Detinna go outside?"

"We have a garden. She'll likely step out at some point."

Tiffany veered the craft. "Scrap the safe house for now. I'm going to have a neighborly talk with Detinna."

"Won't they hear every word?" asked Delphi.

"Trust me, there's a way around everything."

"Wow, did you see that Fifi in the string bikini?"

"Yeah, wish I had a neighbor like her."

"It's nothing like being paid to watch this."

When Detinna went out to the garden a couple of hours later, the neighbor hailed her. The two Watchers focused their listening devices, and the conversation was about plants. There was talk of a new arboretum.

"Wow, that figure won't quit. Make sure you take plenty of pictures."

It was soon over and both women went back inside. "Oh well," said the watcher. "Back to the grind."

A half hour later, the principle left her house and a different crew was left watching. They didn't think much of the lady, who had been wearing the bikini, leaving out of her house later.

"The meeting's been arranged," Tiffany reported. "She wasn't amused about the way I dressed, but she was happy to hear a word about you. I reassured her that the plant was properly cared for, and there were no mishaps."

"Is that all?"

"We talked about a time when orchids are especially aromatic. I'm not sure if she will come to the rendezvous, by her reply. I sensed some hesitancy, but I couldn't place it. We'll know one way or the other tomorrow. If she's on board, we'll attempt the retrieval there and then. You will only have a couple minutes to converse with her before you arouse suspicion."

"How did she look?"

"I don't think there's been enhanced interrogation. She couldn't quite believe that she was out of detention. There's also an underlying sadness. She misses you."

Delphi was left vaguely disturbed. What was his wife's hesitancy? Would she prefer safety to being with him? And if she did, how could she blame her?

Delphi's unease lingered. For some reason, he felt in his gut that Detinna didn't want to join the Resistance. Maybe it was her betrayal early on that prodded that decision. Then, too, he had the added worry. What could she not help but think, after spending days and nights with Tiffany?

Detinna planned her excursion carefully. She continued her morning meanderings, but now included the arboretum in the afternoon. She planted herself within eyeshot of orchids that scented at the times Tiffany had mentioned. The flowers were placed below large palm-leaved plants. She stayed at least two hours so that the Watchers would get bored. At times she would take a break and walk deeper into the arboretum where there were no exits. Sometimes the Watchers didn't follow.

After two days she sensed he was there a moment before she saw him. Delphi was photographing. The moment was awkward because they couldn't speak directly to each other or touch.

"Delphi?" she called in a hushed tone.

He turned slightly to check on a camera setting and put her in his peripheral vision.

"You're in one piece, thank God. I'm supposed to ask if you want to join us. We're ready to take you."

"Do I look older?"

"You look fine."

"Don't you see any difference?"

"You're the same. It's just been a wild three weeks. I want you to be with me."

"Won't you be alright with—"

"How can you say that? There's nothing between Tiffany and I."

"That's not it. I'm pregnant. Four weeks now."

Delphi fought off an impulse to hug her. "Oh my God," he said.

"If I'm on the run, I'll stress and lose the baby. It's better for me to stay home and take my chances."

"But they might pick you back up any time."

"Prison can be low stress. They've been treating me well."

"It's a tactic. Once they find out you're pregnant, they'll try to use that against you."

"I've told them almost everything, anyway. We shouldn't talk much longer. I need to get back. We can't be together... It's for the baby."

Colonel Daniel knew that time was running out. There was still no word of the escapees, and with every passing hour, their chances for a quick retrieval lessened. He had barely been able to hold off the Ruler's order, but his time would be up by the day's end. He reviewed the reports of the watch detail.

There was a reference to a woman sunbathing next door and a conversation. Not unusual for neighbors to talk, but sunbathing? He checked the temperature that day. It was in the upper 60s, not particularly warm. Anomalies.... That was enough to make him question further and check on the neighbor. There was a young woman there, but she had a child six months ago. Would a mother with a newborn be outside sunbathing?

Daniel searched the computer for the transcript on digital file and listened to the conversation. They had already started talking, so the introduction was missing. How much? Inefficiency. The greeting might have given a clue. The two talked about the new arboretum, about flowers. There was even a reference to time and hours.

It was missed. Contact had been made. It was probably already be too late to hold her from going over. He resisted the impulse to send in a full team. If the chance had been missed, questions would be raised, and it would surely seal his fate. He sent in his best five-man team.

The Being had a proper identity created: rich, young, and head of a powerful conglomerate. He took the name Brahman—a bow to his own power and one of world's great religions. His mission was clear, to lure the witch's daughter to the Ruler. After her assent was gained, her youth would be absorbed by the Ruler and she would die. The Victim would sate the Being long enough so that the Ruler, with his renewed power, would provide a renewed supply.

To make the deal, Brahman decided he must first convince the mother of the victim. It would not be easy, and the price would be high. Everyone had their price, and the witch, named Sappho, had been down on her luck lately. Business was slow and her creditors were harrying her.

Later that same day, Sappho was introduced to a potential client. The man who stood before her looked impressive enough, a man of considerable wealth. A luxury car was waiting outside with body guards. He had not engaged in small talk, but immediately stated that he needed an escort for a high official, who would compensate generously. Her daughter would fit his patron's needs. By way of explanation, he mentioned that the official had an interest in the occult.

The witch was discerning and sensed there was something more. "Are you referring to the current Ruler?"

The man hesitated a moment, then answered truthfully. "He has been current for some time."

Sappho smiled. Now, she would surely get a better deal. "Certainly, the emperor"—the witch did not think that the present was much different from ancient times—"doesn't need to come to my humble abode in search of a consort. My daughter Ericka is attractive in her own way and intelligent, but she is not glamourous. Her personality is different—stubborn with a wild streak. She has a few esoteric talents, but surely the emperor has access to better resources."

"Of course, the emperor prefers that his offers to be accepted voluntarily," the man answered with a tone that indicated there was no real choice. "As I have said, he plans to compensate you and your daughter generously. Her tenure of service will be short, not more than a week or two, for the emperor's interests are short term."

The witch quickly moved to negotiation. "What are you offering?"

"Enough to provide a lavish lifestyle for you and your daughter for the rest of your lives. As a bonus, you will be given two young apprentices."

The witch's eyes came alive. It was a hard time, and she was tired of her daughter's sultry ways.

"How do I know all this is real?" she asked, trying to hide her interest.

"You will be given half the payment in money and in persons––a number we can mutually agree upon, but with which you will be pleased. After your daughter's service, you will obtain the other half."

"Why are you asking me?" Sappho decided to ask. "My daughter has turned of age."

"We do not want you to be unhappy. And, as you said, she has a stubborn streak. A word from you.... "

Sappho nodded. Her daughter was an opportunist at heart. Still, she felt something was left unspoken. What was it? The emperor was only a dabbler in the occult....

The man in front of her—who was he, really? With her gaze Sappho tried to look deeper. She saw the constructs of a wealthy entrepreneur who traveled to exotic places, conducted his business and then indulged. She was deflected when she tried to probe further. Could the man have no depth beyond that? *The emptiness of a man of riches . . .* she thought.

"Alright," the witch agreed. "But the price will be high."

"I aim to keep all my clients pleased," the man returned.

CHAPTER XV
A PERSONAL ASSISTANT

Tiffany counted to five. Two at the side entrance and three in front. No other back up was visible. *It must be an elite group,* she thought. *I have to take them all out, or we'll be caught or killed.* Tiffany couldn't count on any real help from Delphi or Detinna. For a moment she considered whether she should just quietly leave. The odds were against her and one's luck only lasted so long.

But Delphi was the leader of the Resistance, and she was his sole bodyguard. It was her duty to protect him. Plus, he had become like a brother due to their shared experience of danger.

The bodyguard decided to take out the side two first, although that might make her too late to protect the principle from the other three. She had the element of surprise.

Tiffany put on a work identification tag and pulled right up as if she had business there. The men watched her carefully as she approached, but she gave no indication other than of being an employee coming to work.

They halted her at the entrance. "Miss, the building is closed. Government inspection for contamination."

The two had let her come too close. One foot swung into groin of the man in front of her, while she slammed the man to the left side in the throat. As the second man gasped for air, she hit the first on the head with her weighted purse, knocking him unconscious. As the other man grabbed for his weapon, Detinna drew hers and fired, sending him into unconsciousness. She quietly went inside, realizing the hard part lay ahead.

Detinna had picked her spot carefully. She glimpsed the three men through the foliage walking down the aisle carefully, scanning the plants.

"They're here," she whispered to Delphi. "Go now. I'll stall them."

Delphi couldn't leave his pregnant wife. "No, we go in together."

"No," said Detinna, ushering him away. "Back and to the right, there's a side exhibit that they won't find right away. Is she close by?"

"Outside."

They entered the rare orchid room. "Here in the corner, behind this trellis, you can lay down. They might not see you. You've got to let me go. They only know I'm here. You know, they can pick me up anytime."

Delphi's reason won over emotion, and he remained hidden as Detinna pulled out her sketch pad and walked over to a group of plants.

Detinna could sense them coming. She halted before a succulent and was already drawing.

"Where is he?" a man asked.

The other two men were already past her.

"Who are you?" she asked.

"Special Police," said the man, not bothering to show identification.

The other two men quickly circled around.

"Maybe he hasn't arrived yet. The guard said four people entered. How many are here?"

"Call the others."

The man called. "No response."

The man instantly grabbed Detinna. "Come with us," he said.

The man named Brahman does not add up, thought Ericka, trying to discern the man before her. He had offered a deal too good to be true. She and her mother would be wealthy for the rest of their lives, and she had only to meet the demands of a high official for a week or two. Her first impulse had been to say no, for something this easy was likely to have a hidden price. She had called upon her mother, but she assured her this was a routine thing among the elite. But why did an elite official choose her?

Ericka wasn't hesitant about offering herself, but there was something about the handsome man that made her wary. His vacuousness was above average, and it hid something. What did she expect? Someone who arranged consorts had long ago left behind their better self in exchange for an easier life.

Ericka asked the man if he had a family.

Brahman raised his eyebrows. "My friends are my family."

Ericka wondered about his answer, which appeared to confirm there was something was amiss. She almost said no then. But her mother knew about such things, and the offer would set them both up for life. It wasn't likely they would ever see such an opportunity again. It could even become the beginning of something more, her entry into powerful circles and an influential life.

Ericka decided. "What do I have to do?"

"Perfect," the man answered. "We'll arrange for transportation tomorrow. Pack lightly and arrange your affairs for a few days."

"Anything special that I should bring?"

The man paused, then said, "No, just yourself."

That's odd. He thought of something but didn't say it, thought Ericka.

To be on the safe side, the witch's daughter decided to bring a few items that would be easy to conceal and help defend herself if necessary.

"Let her go," said Delphi, suddenly appearing. The three special forces men instantly turned, weapons in hand. Detinna was shoved to the side.

"Do not move," they ordered.

"Take me. It's me you want."

The leader of the group motioned with his head, indicating that Detinna could leave.

Detinna couldn't believe what was happening. She would never see him again. "No!" she cried, and she grappled with one of the men.

With an expert move, the man delivered a blow that sent her reeling to the ground. While their attention was focused, they did not notice the entrance of another person. Tiffany got two shots off, knocking their leader unconscious and the one on his right. The third, however, dove behind a concrete raised bed and her third shot was absorbed by the earth.

"Down!" cried Tiffany, and Delphi hit the floor.

It was one against one, and the odds were even at the moment. The man would either use the others as a shield or kill them.

Tiffany had to go on the offensive. It was unexpected and dangerous.

First, she shot out the electrical box, creating sparks and a small fire. Alarms sounded and emergency sprinklers cut on.

Then she rolled, facing the man who had his weapon pointed right at her. They fired simultaneously, and they hit their targets. Both fell.

Delphi rushed to Tiffany. He felt no pulse, then checked her breath.

"Nothing. Breath work. Let me start," said Detinna.

She tried for three minutes. Then Delphi. No results.

Delphi listened for breathing for several seconds more. "Nothing. . ."

"We've lost her," said Detinna. "We've got to go now

Delphi got up, wooden. The impact of her death had almost rendered him immobile.

"Let's go," said Detinna after she shut Tiffany's eyes.

Delphi's survival instinct took hold, and he started moving again. The couple looked at each other and knew. Without protection, their changes of escape were slim.

Ericka waited in the foyer of the Ruler's palace. She had taken care with her dress. She knew the type. They wanted youth, a bit of class, and some spunk, and she could provide this. She would only have to make sure that their side of the deal would be kept. She worried for a moment about what she might have to, but he was a public official. Things would be kept within certain bounds, and he had need for discretion.

The witch's daughter was surprised that she recognized the face of her employer. The Ruler beamed a smile and issued her inside. She hesitated a moment. This was more than she had expected. Why hadn't her mother told her? How could she refuse now? Ericka waited as the Ruler attended to a few things on his console.

"I am looking for a personal assistant," he began. "Someone who will do what is needed for a relatively brief period."

For a moment, she wondered if nothing more would be demanded.

She saw a gleam in his eyes and realized there were unspoken plans. Intuitively, Ericka felt the stakes were high.

"I'm happy to be your personal assistant," she replied. "As for your side of the bargain?"

The Ruler responded lightly. "No one trusts anyone any more. Here are the papers. The documents have been drawn up and signed. You can have it checked out by an independent solicitor."

Ericka's eyes bulged as she considered the figures. If this were true, she and her mother would be quite rich.

Ericka spoke her mind. "How do I know that I won't end up knowing a little too much and being... disposed of?"

The Ruler shrugged off the affront and smiled. "Your own solicitor will know about the agreement. I will not be sharing any confidential material."

Ericka knew that an accident could be arranged with her solicitor. But what choice did she have? One didn't face the Ruler and refuse him. She changed tact.

"I can keep my side of the bargain, if you can keep yours."

The Ruler nodded with a show of relief over his face. Her youth had kicked in. She was either trusting power or feared power. He had wondered for a moment if she already knew too much, for she was the daughter of a psychic.

"I think we can develop a working relationship," said the Ruler.

CHAPTER XVI
FACING THE END

After the news, Daniel drove to the park. The pair had somehow gotten away. Two of his elite team were dead and three more wounded. True, they had taken down the survival expert and the two should be captured shortly. But his time had expired. There were those, no doubt, who were already putting their voice into the Ruler's ear. He did not want to wait to find out what plan was being devised.

Daniel took out a smoke laced with opium. It made him dreamy and toned down his alertness. He reserved this for certain occasions. He thought over his life, his service to the State.

The Head of Security fought off an impulse to run. Maybe, given his skill, he would evade detection for a few days. But in time, they would catch up to him. He even considered for a moment if he should join the Resistance. But even if they accepted him, which was unlikely, he would never be fully trusted.

Daniel inhaled deeply and relaxed. It was easier to leave this life. What was afterwards? He didn't know. He didn't practice religion. He remembered the stories of his grandmother about a world beyond.

In his mind he began to assess his life. He had served the State and done what he had thought was right. What if it was the wrong choice? He had learned to close his eyes too much, he thought. It had started with small things. There was always some justification. At the point that he realized he was doing things he would never had done at the start of his job, it was too late. There was no turning back. *Or was there a choice, even now?*

Daniel saw what appeared to be a dark shadow. He could commit suicide. *No, I can't do that, even if I have chosen what was wrong before.*

The Head of Security heard a click, then turned. His trusted bodyguard was standing outside his car with his weapon drawn.

The expression of the man told him that he took no pleasure in this task.

"I understand," said Daniel, not offering any resistance.

There was a moment of surprise in his bodyguard's face before he extinguished the life of his superior.

Detinna was upset. "You know, it was stupid to show yourself. Your bodyguard is dead. It's just a matter of time before they find us."

"I did what I had to do. I love you."

Detinna smiled. Had she been unreasonable to fear his lack of faithfulness? Delphi had chosen to go with her, even though it had meant he would lose his freedom.

"No use standing around here," she said. "We might as well go on a last ride. Maybe we'll even get lucky."

The couple took out one of the elite team's coded keys and got into one of their vehicles.

"I wish I knew something about survival tactics. She was—" Delphi's voice broke off.

Detinna understood. "I'm really sorry about Tiffany. She did her duty to the end. But we have to survive without her now. Maybe there is a way for us."

Delphi turned off the transponder, veered the vehicle around, and said, "I've got an idea."

"You're going to back to our house?" asked Detinna after Delphi punched in directions.

"Not quite, but the idea is like that, to hide in plain sight."

"Won't turning off the transponder start an alarm?"

"Statistically, a lot goes off and on all the time. They'll likely have to run down too many before they find this one, and by that time, we'll be somewhere else."

A few minutes later, Delphi ditched the vehicle in a public lot. Then they took public transportation to a familiar neighborhood.

As they walked down a street, Detinna smiled. "The Time Expansion folks? Are they still in business?"

"Let's find out."

They were greeted by Alice, who expressed surprise and concern.

"Come in," said Alice without hesitation. "You're just in time for some afternoon tea in the sun room."

"We don't mean to be inconvenient," said Detinna.

"No, not all," Dr. Burgess reassured, who had come at the sound of their voices. "I'm sure the party we're expecting won't mind meeting you."

The Ruler felt a hint of pressure on his throat. "Why do you delay?" asked the Being, whose hunger had grown. "Maybe you are ready to die?"

"No, no . . .this takes time," said the Ruler. "You want a willing sacrifice, and I will find a sweet one."

"Three days," said the Being. "You know where the table is."

"It hasn't been used for some time."

The pressure in his throat increased. "Full ritual. Twelve witnesses."

The Ruler did not want his private dealings brought before the mystic priesthood. "Are you—"

The rest of his sentence made no sound. "Do it," ordered the Being.

The next morning the Ruler had a headache. He had just reviewed the morning security briefing, headlined by a piece of news. The Director of Operations had been found dead in the park, a reported suicide. He wondered about his decision. Daniel had been competent and faithful, but he wasn't getting results at this critical time. Speed was of the essence. With a lucky stroke, the Resistance might still catch the empire off balance. He couldn't allow that to happen.

There was no question about the efficiency of the new Director of Security, although the look in his eyes was disturbing. Gorgon would do anything to anyone, as long as he was ordered, and it helped secure his position.

"Give me the breakdown," asked the Ruler.

"Subjects whereabouts unknown at present. The Security Vehicle they used has been found. We can't be far behind them. We have questioned the three who survived, but there wasn't much of value."

"Dispose of them. No loose ends."

Gorgon barked a coded order over a communicator, then said, "It's done."

The Ruler winced. Gorgon could have waited until their conversation was over, but he was not known for delaying orders.

"What about the bodyguard?"

"Her body was removed by the Resistance before back up arrived. They are funny about leaving bodies behind."

The Ruler returned to the matter at hand. "How long do you project it will take to find the two?"

"Within 24 hours. Maybe 48 hours, if they manage to find help."

"Three days then," said the Ruler. "Time is running out."

Gorgon remained standing, although the Ruler had signaled that the conversation was over.

"What is it?"

"Do you want them taken alive?"

The Ruler hesitated. "The woman is no longer needed. But there is something I need to ask the new leader of the Resistance."

Ericka noted the guards outside the door. Was that really necessary? Did the Ruler really think that she was going to flee and renege on her part of the bargain? One did not go back on their agreement with the most powerful man in the world.

Her mother had given approval, but had she really looked out for her interest? Ericka wondered if she should have talked to her mother face to face. Then she could have read the truth on such a serious matter. There was no time for that now. The first appointment, a dinner, would start within the hour, and it would be a private affair.

Ericka only had to survive for so long. Still, she was uncertain and wondered what would happen if she didn't please him. She had not left herself defenseless. They had not quite searched her thoroughly enough.

"We didn't expect to see you here again," said Dr. Burgess as he poured tea. "You've being sported on the Tele as a dangerous terrorist, as one who would unravel the whole fabric of society. Why did you come here?"

"We thought they might not be expecting us to go to anywhere so obvious," answered Delphi.

"But they will eventually check here. That being said, I suspect we have a little more time."

"Is the movement collapsing?" Detinna asked.

"Partly," Alice responded. "We have a second plan in place, and you both can have a role in it."

"I don't think we're quite prepared for this," Delphi responded.

"We know," said Dr. Burgess. "But Vance chose you for good reason. The Ruler has an obsessive interest in gaining immortality, and he thinks that you have something to offer in that regard. We are hoping to exploit that interest. You have already helped to eliminate one of our most dangerous adversaries."

"Who?" asked Delphi.

"The Head of Security—the one in charge of finding you—was reported to have committed suicide yesterday."

"That was Tiffany's doing. She... " Delphi, surprised by his sudden grief, couldn't continue.

"Yes, she was one of our best," said Alice. "Some thought that Vance should have left her in charge of the Resistance. But she was young yet, and we needed her for special assignments. It's a loss here for everyone."

There was a moment of shared grief, then Dr. Burgess spoke. "We have limited time. You shouldn't stay here for more than an hour. The plan is for Delphi to offer to meet the Ruler in order to negotiate a truce."

"I'm not an assassin," said Delphi.

"We are only asking for you to help create a diversion," Alice clarified. "You will need to make physical contact."

"I still don't understand that," said Delphi. "I don't have mystical powers."

"Whether you do or not, your touch will distract the Ruler at a critical time," said Dr. Burgess. "As you've been told, there are reasons for this in his psychology."

"And perhaps you underestimate the influence of the other world, which sometimes works through touch," Clare added. "Did you ever touch the Time Thief?"

"No—well, there was a moment when it seemed that something dissolved in him. I don't know what it was, but it felt like he spilled over me."

Everyone looked up at Delphi. "Does that mean something?"

No one answered Delphi's question, but it led Detinna to ask, "Does that mean the Ruler is living on stolen time?"

"You can say that," answered Dr. Burgess. "We believe he has had three extensions already. A fourth will consolidate his power such that resistance will be almost impossible. Yet, this also brings us hope."

"Hope?" asked Delphi.

"That he will be blinded by his desire and be willing to meet with you. The risk will be high for you, but higher for all if you don't succeed."

"What of the Ruler himself?" asked Detinna. "Is there any hope that he might change and negotiate in good faith?"

Dr. Burgess sighed. "I forget that your weakness has served to help us. We are not ministers, but revolutionaries. We want a more just world, and if that means letting evil people go more hurriedly to their own death, we do not interfere."

The guest that Dr. Burgess and Alice were expecting arrived. It was a man who was fit and professional, although not easy to place. He held a brief private conversation with Dr. Burgess.

"Are you a survival expert?" guessed Delphi when the man joined them.

Dr. Burgess answered. "Mark could serve as Tiffany's replacement, but I'm afraid that even a full detail won't enable you to last long on the outside."

"So what is the Resistance going to do next?" asked Delphi.

"We're awaiting your orders."

"Orders? You mean you're taking this Leader of the Resistance thing seriously?"

Dr. Burgess nodded, and Mark handed him a packet. "Here's the plan. We have people in place at strategic points. You just need to review it, OK it, then set the time."

"Set the time? You mean, there really is a chance?"

"None of us knew how much was in place," admitted Dr. Burgess. "We have sufficient forces left at critical places, if their response can be hampered…. We'll have to throw everything at once, as well. We don't have much time, however. We need to decide on things here and now."

Delphi looked at Detinna. "So we'd be fully in?" asked Detinna.

"I think we are already in a few times over."

WORD CAME SOONER THAN expected. Dinner just beyond the door in her room. Ericka hadn't really noticed the door before. It appeared to be a decorative door. She wore a white and loose-fitting garment they had given her to wear.

Ericka wondered what she would do with her poison capsule. It was flesh colored and missed in the search. If they detected it, no doubt she would be killed. She wondered what good it would do her. Either she could commit suicide to evade whatever was planned, or somehow manage to have revenge on the Ruler, then die. Maybe she wouldn't need to use it all.

She wondered what the Ruler would do with her after her service was completed. Would he really let her go, or arrange an untimely accident?

The temperature seemed hot. Maybe that was the way the Ruler liked it. He was older, after all. Ericka could think of no chance for her survival unless the Ruler allowed it, so she must please him. She left the poison pill behind in the bathroom. A week or two wouldn't be that long. Maybe she had exaggerated the danger. The door opened. It was about to begin.

CHAPTER XVII
END GAME

Delphi and Detinna studied the plans in silence. It called for simultaneous attacks on multiple nerve centers. Casualties would be high, projected in the thousands.

"I didn't know the Resistance had this capability," said Delphi, trying to hide his astonishment. "Why is the timing, my decision?"

"Vance trusted you. Whether this succeeds or not depends on timing and your efforts to divert the ruler."

"Well, I hate to ask, but how can am I supposed to know when? And won't he merely put me on hold, when the crisis starts?"

"Our intelligence reveals that he becomes obsessed and goes into these thought reveries about immortality. Even if he is able to snap out of it, we can count on his judgement being clouded. Your job is to put him in that altered state."

"And what if I fail?"

"Then we will all likely fail"

"And you really think he will see me on demand?"

"It is likely, for you are the leader of the Resistance, after all. But the most important factor is that he believes you know how to reverse the flow of time."

"I don't really have a cure for time, except to find another Time Thief who took years and is willing to die," said Delphi, looking again at the plans for attack. "How many innocents will die?"

"Certainly hundreds, maybe thousands. The government will probably make indiscriminate reprisals to deter us."

"And what of deaths afterwards?"

"Unknown for the immediate future, but there will no doubt be more death. We do know, however, of secret cleansing plans to rid the society of elements that are related in any way to the Resistance. We can't afford not to act."

Delphi felt resigned. "What type of timetable are we talking about for this meeting?"

"We can maintain things in place for maybe three or four days. That's the window. If we pass up this chance, it may be years before another like it appears. It's your decision when you go, and we'll take that as our cue."

"I feel like there's something being left out."

"There usually is. It's a safety consideration for survival. Not all our resources are listed here. Not all the moves against the Ruler either…. But it's best not to know what you don't need to know," said Dr. Burgess.

"Speaking of contingencies, what if the Ruler is captured or killed?"

"The odds of collapse go markedly in our favor. The Ruler has not made provisions other than to renew himself for now. There are three or four others who would likely vie for immediate control. That would take time to resolve and during that time we will likely complete our plans."

"One more thing," Delphi thought to say. "About my survival. The plans are rather high risk for me, personally."

Neither Dr. Burgess and Alice offered any disagreement. "You're our best hope," Alice simply said.

"Welcome," said the Ruler, wearing a faint smile and his formal attire. It seemed incongruous.

"Is this a state dinner?" Ericka chided.

The Ruler's eyes narrowed for a moment. He would not be so easily thrown out of his good mood, however.

"No, you're the only guest," he answered, widening his smile.

"Is there an event afterwards?" Ericka pursued, and she thought she saw the slightest tightening around his lips.

"I've come from an official event and haven't had time to change," he lied.

Ericka was about to ask another question, but refrained. What difference does it make *why* he dressed up? Maybe he was simply trying to look good, or maybe it was his way of showing his power and her powerlessness.

Ericka glanced around the room at a fireplace with an old fashioned wood frame, a red couch, antiques, and a door near the middle of the room that seemed out of place. *What's beyond the door?* she wondered.

The Ruler noticed her questioning look, but tried to make chit chat.

What's he avoiding? she wondered. It was painful being a psychic, where one usually sensed several steps ahead. Although she could be wrong, and it would cause needless anxiety, often—enough times—she was spot on. And when you're right, the inevitable thought follows: *Why didn't I do something about that beforehand?* Now it didn't seem to matter, for she had little or no power to control things. Ericka tried for a moment to see behind the door, but sensed only darkness beyond. *It's night outside.*

The Ruler continued to make small talk, and she obliged. She even giggled in a flirty way. She might as well enjoy herself. He was not unhandsome, although older, and he exuded power. The Ruler, no doubt, would forget her soon after he got what he wanted. If all went well, it would be worth it.

"Where's the bedroom?" she suddenly asked.

The Ruler's eyes evidenced a faint surprise, but he nodded toward the door.

"Can I see it?" asked Ericka, springing up.

"No," the Ruler ordered with sudden authority. Then his voice became mild. "Let's finish our meal and enjoy the fireplace."

Ericka sat back down, showing a pout. Maybe she should be acting more immature. She would be more likely to catch him off guard.

"Don't you think it's a little much, having guards search me?"

"I apologize. It's a standard precaution with anyone who contacts my person."

"Well, there hasn't been much contact so far. This is boring."

"Have another glass of wine," he replied.

They were drinking from the same bottle, so she hadn't thought to refuse. Wine made everything easier.

After dinner they moved to the couch, and he put his arm around her. She pretended to be interested and made a point of toying with his shirt.

"Oh, I've got to pee," she said suddenly and before he could respond, she went out to her r room.

The door had been locked, but the Ruler pressed a button which allowed her to go. A male and female guard were on either side of the door.

A couple of minutes later, she came out with a quirky smile. "Why not let the handsome hunk clear me?" The male guard searched her.

When Ericka sat back on the couch, the Ruler was on the communicator. "You promised no business calls," she said, pouting.

She could hear pieces of sentences from his earpiece. It was louder than usual due to the Ruler's age. ".... immediate information ... only talk to you."

The emperor smiled, then got up and said, "Sorry, this will only take a few minutes. Wait for me"

Ericka showed the largest pout she could. "What could be that important?"

"I'll be back shortly."

"I'll lose the mood. I won't feel like it!"

"Why don't you have dessert?" asked the Ruler, eyeing the tart, then proceeding to step out.

"I'd like ice cream topped with jelly beans," Ericka declared/ "Or I'm leaving now!"

The Ruler turned. "No problem. I'll order it."

CHAPTER XVIII
YOUTH TAKER

Dr. Burgess heard the pleas of the witch, a free-lance occultist named Sappho, who was not a member of any group. She was dressed in black formal wear, and her face was visibly distressed. Her daughter was in danger. She could provide valuable assistance to the Resistance, if they would only help her. The witch had word through her occult connections that there was to be a sacrifice, and the Ruler was involved. Her daughter had already signed a contract. She added two plus two. She should have seen it coming. Now, she must do what she could to save her daughter. The Resistance was the logical, if highly risky, place to start. She knew that the Time Expansion Center had connections.

Dr. Burgess let the witch plead her case. She did so, it seemed, with a sense that she had already lost her daughter, and that this was a long shot at best.

"A sacrifice?" asked Delphi.

"I have heard that you are not a novice to the other world. Perhaps you know there are spirits who hunger across worlds and who are always wanting victims. Powerful people can provide victims. Please, help my daughter. Perhaps you have a way to access the Ruler."

Dr. Burgess shot a questioning glance to the Delphi. It was his decision. Delphi wondered if it added an unnecessary complication and whether the witch was legitimate. But the plea sounded genuine and urgent.

Was this the cue they were waiting for? wondered Delphi. *Yet another distraction . . .* "Perhaps we can add you to our plans. If – "

Sappho interrupted. "There's no time for elaborate plans. It's happening tonight."

"It would not be easy to be put on the Ruler's calendar on the same day," Dr. Burgess remarked.

"You can launch a strike. You can parley with him."

"What help can you provide us?" asked Delphi.

"I can be of use in the other world. An unseen battle is always being fought there. In this matter, it would help to have at least one other with me."

"Alright, we'll consider," Delphi answered, signaling the witch to step aside.

"The time has arrived," said Alice. "The emperor will already be distracted by the sacrifice. That intelligence alone is worth a lot."

Everyone agreed.

"So Delphi, you should try to see the Ruler tonight," said Dr. Burgess. "Tell his aides that you are willing to offer him youth in exchange for a truce in this war."

Delphi nodded. Things seemed to be coming to together.

"Will this put a halt to his designs on Sappho's daughter?" asked Detinna.

"If we are completely successful," answered Dr. Burgess. "There will be no more Ruler. But there remains one more matter."

"Yes," continued Alice. "The witch has asked for help. The question is who has the most experience."

"I think I do," said Detinna.

"You can't," protested Delphi. "You're expecting our child."

"It's alright," said Detinna. "If this plan doesn't succeed, there won't be any future for our child."

After a long pause, Dr. Burgess said, "If Delphi approves, we'll send a communication to the Ruler."

Delphi weighed everything and felt a premonition that it was likely that someone would die on the mission. But what was the alternative? If they did nothing, they would all be at the mercy of the State, and there would be no mercy.

Delphi hugged Detinna and whispered, "Good luck. I'll always love you."

"I love you too," she answered, reading his eyes. "Don't worry, we'll see each other again."

"Let's go," said Delphi.

The Being felt satisfaction with the progress in its plans. Its hunger, however, had grown so intense lately that it was converting to a rage toward all living things. It would be satisfied it knew, but it knew, that even after feasting, the hunger would not completely go away. It would start gnawing at him shortly afterwards, such that his satisfaction would be short lived.

If it had the entire world, a limitless supply of victims, then maybe the hunger would go away, it reasoned. For now, it needed but one to ensnare the emperor fully. Then it would be provided with routine victims. One could not obtain that much power without having to feed the beast that gave it.

The Being looked into the future and saw its dying victims bleeding, hanging, and crying for mercy. But their pleas were only a whispering compared to the roar of the hunger within it.

DETINNA WAS IN THE grotto for only a moment before she felt that the world was slipping by her. *The witch really knows her stuff,* she thought. *I just said that I was ready and we're already moving.*

After a brief span that covered an immense space, they came to a room unlike any Detinna had seen, a pitch dark chamber lit by eyes in a circle. The eyes, paradoxically, cast a dark light that sought to bind things. Hooded, sexless figures were about to perform a ritual. A table or altar, made of white marble with swirls of black, was lit by candles that seemed to feed the blackish light. At times the candles glittered and Detinna wondered how.

One of the figures shifted, as if sensing their presence. Detinna saw an impression of a face—if face it was—devoid of expression and seeming to absorb all expression. The figure's cape bore a red slash across its left shoulder. For a moment its gaze turned toward them, but its sightless eyes gazed past them. Somehow, the witch was able to shroud them. Still, Detinna read a raw menace behind the eyes. She became fearful and looked to Sappho, whose calm face bore an intensity that took in all that was happening.

"The door," the witch whispered. "My daughter is behind the door."

"Yes, I can see outlines. What can we do?"

"Nothing for now. They stand in the way. The leaders of the Occult gather for a feeding once a year."

"Can they see us? Their faces aren't visible."

"No. Their attention is focused elsewhere. Perhaps they could if they all tried at once. But their hunger absorbs them. For some reason they have been kept waiting longer than usual. I must try to keep my daughter from being captured by their gaze when she comes in, but I don't know how."

A few moments later, the door opened and her daughter appeared in a white, diaphanous gown. She was in a drowsy, dreamlike state.

A man, formally dressed—the Ruler—escorted her to a table at the center of the circle. He helped her lay down, pulled out a silver knife and laid it next to her.

It's true, thought Detinna. *They are really going to sacrifice her.* The witch's grim look confirmed her powerlessness.

The Ruler hovered over Ericka and began reciting something as if he were a priest. For a moment Ericka held out her hand as if grasping at something.

Detinna felt a pain stab in her chest. "Isn't there anything we can do?"

"Too late," the witch responded, with steel in her voice. "We may be able to spare her body from being violated afterwards."

Delphi couldn't quite believe that he would actually have face time with the Ruler. He wondered if he could engross the Ruler for long. Did he really believe that he could grant him a new lease on life? And if he was able to make physical contact, what difference would that make?

The Ruler already appeared preoccupied, but his gaze came around and focused on him. Delphi felt a sudden importance and resisted an impulse to reach out and offer his hand. A red laser light on his chest was warning not to make sudden moves against the person of the Ruler.

"So you're the new Leader of the Resistance, the one who stole back time from the Time Thief," began the Ruler, surveying Delphi with intensity.

"Yes to both," said Delphi, returning the Ruler's gaze. They locked, and neither sensed an advantage.

"Your advance people said you have an offer for me."

"Yes, a cessation of hostilities and a negotiated truce for an advanced technique which may be of use to you."

"I'm listening."

Delphi suddenly decided to offer a caveat. "I must warn you that although you might succeed in gaining youth, there are still complications from growing old inside. There is an advanced spiritual technique for internal renewal, which we could include as part of the package."

The Ruler was instantly annoyed. "I've not come here for spiritual improvement. Do you know the Time Thief's method or not?"

"In the end, you must know that the spirits will exact their price," Delphi rejoined.

The Ruler wondered at this, something he had kept mostly hidden from himself, then gave his reasoning. "The end is distant and my gain immediate. What others realize when it's too late in life, I'll know while I'm young. We are uncertain of what is beyond this life. But I am not here to talk metaphysics. Tell me the method."

"You have no qualms at being a time vampire"

"Do not delay me with moral quibbles. Do you have the goods or not?"

"The witch's daughter. She is more than a name."

The Ruler's eyebrows raised. "How do you know about her?"

"Our techniques are not limited to Time Theft."

For a moment the Ruler wondered if the witch's daughter could be a plant. But the pick was wholly his, and they couldn't have known.

"I will return to this later," said the Ruler, getting up. "Maybe you have something for me, maybe not. Consider yourself lucky that I am not trying to find out by the usual techniques."

Delphi tried to hide the sunken feeling that he had failed to engross the Ruler for very long. He suddenly extended his hand to shake—an archaic custom. The Ruler had lived back to a time when handshakes were routinely exchanged, and in his haste accepted Delphi's hand. For a moment, he paused at this oddity, then ordered his guards with a signal to detain Delphi. The Ruler turned on his heels and left.

The Ruler had felt a slight charge with the shake. He knew that this was simply static electricity. Could he have been slipped something? He instinctively looked at his hand. There were no marks. It was foolish to think that it was possible. But he had been touched. The man was relatively young, but he had been older once, according to the report. *Did that mean that the touch would work against him?* wondered the Ruler. He shook off the confusion.

The Ruler found himself thinking more about at the encounter. Did the Leader of the Resistance really think that he could convert him? Things were set in motion long ago and there was no stopping it. It would have been nice if he had offered an easier way, but he sensed that the new leader of the Resistance was bluffing. The Ruler would, as he had always done before, ruthlessly accomplish his objectives. The Resistance would be totally wiped out, and he would satisfy the dark Being with a sacrifice that would give him a new lease on life. No doubt, his associates will be surprised to see him young once more, and some would even doubt that it was he. But his immediate circle had been forewarned of the impending miracle. Few would contest the result when the last of the Resistance was eliminated.

He hastened to the matter of the witch's daughter. The Ruler had actually found himself attracted. In another time, he might have kept her as one of his paramours. As it was, there wasn't time for a substitute and arrangements had been finalized.

The Ruler wished for a moment that the circle would not be present to feed their dark desires. He took little pleasure in the ritual or in the killing itself. He only wanted youth.

There remained the supposed problem of making her a willing victim, but that could be easily solved. He would slip her a drug that would render her non-resistant. As he poured the drink, that he felt a dull but sudden pain in the back of his neck. *These aches and pains will soon be gone,* he thought.

"Why did you leave me?" Ericka mock whined. "It must have been important. I hope no one will interrupt us now. I hope it's nothing to do with those Resistance people either. They keep upsetting things. "

She splashed a kiss on the Ruler, and pressed against his side that held his knife. He looked at her face, but saw no cause for alarm.

Still, the Ruler felt disconcerted for a moment. Had she known about Delphi? Her mind appeared distant. She was enjoying the last of her ice cream and toppings. "Aren't you having any dessert," she said, kissing him again.

A bell gonged, and the Ruler startled ever so slightly. "It's time...."

"What? It's midnight? How romantic," she purred.

"Time for one more drink," said the Ruler. He got up and noticed how heavy his body felt. *The sacrifice will come none too soon,* he thought.

The Ruler set two goblets filled with a red liquor in front of them.

"It's so rich," said Ericka. "I think I've had enough dessert."

"One last toast," the Ruler insisted. "I'm sure you will find this drink most exquisite."

Ericka raised the glass and drank. It tasted like sweet fire.

"Good, we're ready," said the Ruler.

The drug took almost immediate effect. Ericka's eyes opened wide in alarm for a moment, then became a haze. The Ruler knew that he had only to give a suggestion and she would obey. The highly classified drug worked well, if for only thirty minutes.

"Come with me," he ordered, standing up.

Surprisingly, she responded, "You haven't had yours?" *How does she have the strength to summon an independent thought?* the Ruler wondered. *Had they underestimated the dosing?*

"I'll pass for now. Keeping myself trim.... "

"Just a taste of this ice cream fudge and jelly beans then," she said, kissing him again. "Would you like one?"

"Yum, good," he said, waiting for the drug to work fully.

A moment later, her pupils were fully enlarged. "It's time to get up," he ordered.

Ericka stood up docilely. The door swung open, and they were greeted by the circle of unmoving caped figures.

The Ruler suppressed a shudder when he saw the priests' cold, death-dealing eyes. He knew that he was safe as long as he did his part. He had no intention of breaking protocol.

The Ruler moved a little woodenly. *These rituals have a way of taking something out of you.* He took no delight in preforming the sacrifice, but it worked and it kept the High Priests and priestesses satisfied.

"Lay down on top of here," directed the Ruler.

"Why here?" Ericka asked without stopping.

Again, the Ruler wondered at the drug's efficacy. Her face, however, did not wait for a response and she lay down.

The Ruler said to her. "The experience won't be like anything you've had before."

"That's good," said Ericka without a smile. The drug was now in full effect.

"The knife will greet your heart and you will die," he said.

"Yes," she answered, without any hint of resistance.

"Good. I am glad you are willing."

"I am willing," she repeated.

The Ruler looked at his hand that held the knife. The wrinkles seemed to join the ivory carvings like his knife and hand were one. *Soon I will be young again,* thought the Ruler.

The drug had been more powerful than Ericka had expected. She had taken an all-purpose antidote that worked against most common sedatives, but this drug was uncommonly powerful. There was a numbing sensation that overtook her from head to toe. With a sudden clarity, she realized she would not likely to get away with her life.

Ericka could not stop herself from sleep-walking into the circle of hooded figures. She should be afraid, she realized, but she wasn't. The drug, mercifully, had taken that away too. She would do just as asked. *Yes, there is the table and the knife ... that's good.*

Ericka remembered she had taken another precaution, but she couldn't remember what. She sensed two other presences in the chamber, which also brought a moment of confusion. She had managed to move her head, but saw no one.

I'm too young to die.... Why didn't I see this coming? Why didn't my mother warn me? She had heard stories about the youth-takers and occult rituals, but they were considered to be rare and fringe practices, not found in the heart of empire.

While I still have some mind left ... what can I do? Nothing—only observe my end.

The Ruler helped her lay down, then proceeded to place a ritual garb on.

Where would he strike her? Yes, the heart. At least, it will be quick.

CHAPTER XIX
THE SACRIFICE

Detinna was horrified that she could do nothing to stop a human sacrifice. Her spirit body appeared not to have traction in this dark chamber except to see and hear. Still, she instinctively found herself moving toward the victim. As the witch's daughter was laid on the table, Detinna sensed a sudden flow of energy from the hooded man with the red slash. Yes, he would first absorb her life.

Sappho, sensing Detinna's intention, cried out, "Don't! There is far too much power here. There's nothing we can do to stop it."

Detinna turned. "I can't just watch."

"We can save her body afterwards."

"Who are these wicked people?"

"It doesn't matter who, although they were persons once. They're now called *Feeders*."

Detinna realized she was only being stalled, and there wasn't much time. She resumed her approach.

Sappho followed for a space, before saying. "I can no longer go with you. Our spirit bodies will become visible. They have too much power for you to stop them!"

Detinna saw the eyes of Red Slash first. The eyes, cold and cruel, glanced in her direction. It was only for a moment. After he perceived no threat, he returned to the victim.

"Why?" she asked, directing her voice toward him.

The eyes instantly turned her way. The eyes were searing, pinning her. "How dare you intrude upon the ceremony?" he demanded.

"You must stop," said Detinna, willing it with all her power. She stared at the Ruler, who was gripping the silver knife.

"A double feast!" Red Slash exclaimed as the space around Detinna tightened.

"Withdraw or your life will be forfeit," cried Sappho. "My daughter's life is gone!"

For a moment, Detinna wavered. She had almost taken a step back when she saw the victim raise her hand for help. Detinna cried out the name of the Being. As if by command, the forces around Ericka lifted and swirled around Detinna.

As the power of the twelve clamped on her, Detinna saw the lineaments of her body form. A few feet away, the Ruler raised his knife and waited for the signal.

The eyes of Red Slash were fully locked on Detinna, and a gray, cloud-like hand clutched her spirit throat.

Detinna gasped, her head whirled as she faced her end. Then she saw something that did not seem possible. The Ruler collapsed atop his victim.

In the instant that the Ruler clutched his throat, he realized what had happened. *It was the jellybean! It had gone back and forth between us.* She had caressed him, he had lost focus, and the poisoned jellybean went down.

How could the witch's daughter outfox me? How could I have been so foolish? There was no time for further self recriminations. He was dying. The Ruler saw Ericka's dazed face and her faint smile. She would live, if only for a few moments longer than him.

The Ruler had one last act. He stuttered out the Being's name, then collapsed upon the woman. He had become the sacrifice.

Ericka waited calmly for her end. She said a prayer of sorts and silent goodbyes to the people she cared for. Her eyes teared for her own unlived future. Her life would be over before it had really begun.

Perhaps the hardest thing for her to endure was that the one who had given her life had participated in it.

Ericka sensed the two presences beyond the harsh circle. They wanted to help her, but hadn't the power to break through the circle. She would die.

Ericka heard herself obeying the commands to lie atop the table and to say she was willing. It was painless as the death itself would be.

It was only when she saw the Ruler clutch his throat that the memory came back to her of the poisoned pill. So she would have her revenge. The other hooded figures or the guards would surely kill her, but the Ruler wouldn't live longer than her.

His body fell hard and knocked out her breath. Then all the gazes of the circle bore down upon her and tried to crush her. The drug had worn off, and she was able to lift her head. Then the twelve's focus suddenly shifted as another presence approached. An unknown woman was coming for her.

Ericka managed to shrug out from under the Ruler's body, which seemed to have become lighter. She was amazed at how thin and gray he appeared in death. She saw that the unknown woman had placed herself between her and the circle. The woman was fearless, but clearly out powered.

The hooded figure had no need of a weapon. He would use his hands to snuff out the woman's life.

No, she mustn't die. thought Ericka, moving toward them. It was too late. The woman had already fallen into the hands of the dark, scarlet figure. There was nothing to do but to try to save herself. Just as the other hooded figures began to turn their gazes, Ericka slipped out the door. The impact of the spirit eyes on the closed door sounded like a crack of a whip.

Red Slash could no longer control his hunger. Seeing the expected sacrifice had failed, he loosened his fury on the interloper. It was not the one he envisioned, but it was better to have half-foods, than none at all. As for the Being, perhaps it would be sated with the Ruler. After all, the Ruler had called its name, a sign of willingness.

The witch saw that her daughter had escaped for the moment and that Detinna had sacrificed herself. But Red Slash, in his feeding, had made a costly mistake. He had disregarded her and underestimated her presence. She was not equal to his power, but with the element of surprise and because he was sated from the feast, she could fell him.

The witch focused her eyes and seared his spirit being. As her spirit clawed at him, he cried in pain and tried to redirect his fury upon her, but it was too late. His being imploded and fragments of himself were cast out, each containing a partial consciousness. His power was reduced to causing pinpricks or rashes, for he had become a minor demon.

Sappho could not believe that her daughter survived, and that Detinna had died. Somehow, the Ruler had been killed too, and the hooded figures were gone as well.

Ericka saw the surprise on the handler's faces when she walked back into the room. They secured her, rushed past her, and felt for the Ruler's pulse. As they attended him, an alarm sounded from outside. The empire was under attack.

CHAPTER XX
FINAL DECISION

The new head of security, Evak, evaluated the rapidly evolving situation. The Ruler had died and there was no obvious second. The Resistance was mounting a series of strategic attacks that were expanding by the moment. The Resistance had finally shown its hand—which was surprising in its strength—and had chosen the moment well. Whoever had organized this should not to be underestimated. He, however, had prepared for this contingency.

He would temporarily take command. But the larger question was unresolved: who would be the next Ruler? There would be competing factions, and it would be messy after the Resistance was stamped out. A lot of people would die and large numbers would be imprisoned. But this deed, her foresaw, would also likely sow the seeds for the empire's future demise. Was there any way around this?

Evak realized that he, himself, could become the new Ruler. He would simply, while he held power, kill off all possibles, then institute a period of reform and gain popular support. Gradually, the old ways of empire would return as he clung to power. He had seen this happen to the Ruler, after his first round of youth.

Evak's lieutenants were awaiting his orders. It would take no more than an hour to secure his position. The Resistance would gain ground, but only for a time. There was also the so-called Leader of the Resistance, whom they had captured. This loose end might prove useful.

"Bring me the man called Delphi," Evak ordered, to the surprise of his subordinates.

Dr. Burgess and Alice, relocated at a safe house, received the latest word. After some initial successes, the Resistance were failing. At first, the news had been too good to be true. The Ruler had somehow been killed. The opening had been wide. The State's security forces, however, had proven more tough and resilient than expected. They had held off attacks on all fronts. A relative unknown subordinate, named Evak, had proved himself surprisingly capable, and would likely emerge as the new Ruler.

Still, there was a chance. It would take an awful lot of luck.

Dr. Burgess and Alice deeply regretted the death of Detinna, news they had gained after Sappho returned. The Resistance was used to causalities, but they had known Detinna well and she held a special role.

Delphi had succeeded in his mission, but he was—as expected—captured. A decision now depended upon Dr. Burgess. No doubt, the Special Police would be picking up all Resistance members and would, in all likelihood, execute them.

Dr. Burgess turned to Mark and asked, "Do we have any chance of escape?"

"Little or none. The State's forces have paused to regroup. They don't realize we've already thrown our best punch. "

"Fail safe option?" he asked.

"We have pills... I think it's best to use them. The outlier sectors might survive to fight another day."

Dr. Burgess turned to Alice, "There is an escape plan that is best taken by one. I have a packet with the necessary documents for you."

"No, I'll die with you," said Alice. "It will protect others for I know too much. I wouldn't want to be in this world without you, anyway."

"What do you mean *without me?* You mean—"

"You didn't know?"

Dr. Burgess gazed into Alice's eyes for a few moments, then said, "I guess I did. Alright. We'll wait until they approach." The two held each other.

Evak found Delphi calm and unperturbed for being a prisoner.

"The attempted overthrow by the Resistance has failed," he began. "It's just a matter of time. I am asking that you assist us in shutting down the fighting, to minimize causalities."

"She died," said Delphi. "I felt it."

Although Evak was not known as particularly empathic, he offered condolences. After all, the man's wife had died. The acting Ruler's next words surprised Delphi. "Although our victory is assured, things have changed. Your recruit killed the Ruler and did us an unwitting favor. The leader of the occult has disappeared. It was he who infected our empire and controlled things behind the scenes."

Delphi nodded blankly.

"Let me make my request again. If you encourage a quick surrender, we can save lives on all sides."

"Surely, command of the Resistance has passed," Delphi mumbled.

"We can put you on the Tele."

"So you would be anointed all the sooner? The occult will eventually regroup and demand more sacrifices. Are you ready for their demands?"

"I am very efficient in this world," Evak replied, "and I know a little of the other. It seems though, that you have more of a knack for it. Perhaps you and I could work together. The woman who killed the Ruler could also prove useful."

Delphi paused. Would he sell out and become part of the new order? Detinna had died, and he had nothing to go back to. This man, Evak, seemed to have a human streak in him. He regretted losing unnecessary life.

But there was always a price. In whatever position they would give him, he would be watched and controlled. He would be a bone to be thrown to the side if need be. He might fake it for a while, but he would not be his own person.

"No," Delphi replied. "I can't be a part of any more killing. It's better not to live."

"Look," Evak said suddenly sounding earnest.

A sudden communication indicating trouble in one of the sectors came through. "Contain it at all costs," Evak ordered.

"Should we firestorm the central rebel civilian sectors for complete elimination?" the voice asked.

"Hold for five minutes." said Evak who turned to Delphi. "Help me. The decision is yours."

"Maybe it would save some lives now, but how many more will be lost in the future if the empire continues decades more? How long before I'm no longer necessary, and you dispense with me?"

"You don't understand me. I'm a good security man and don't aspire to anything more. I am asking for you to become the new Ruler."

Detinna had felt the sudden fury of the witch, ripping through the hooded figure's defenses. Then suddenly he was gone, fragmented into thousands of globules that kept getting smaller. It was too late for her, however.

Or was it? The Being behind all this violence was nearby, she sensed, shapeless yet brooding. "You need not die," said the Being. "I am rich in time."

"It is a gift, not without strings," she answered.

"Yes, service is required. Isn't it true in your world, that you must work for what you get?"

"Did you work for the time you have or did you steal it?"

"What do you know of my world or of time?" asked the Being. "I am your only hope before your consciousness becomes extinguished forever."

What if it was? Detinna asked herself. *Wouldn't any life, even if it were compromised, be better than nothing?*

"I have seen a tunnel of light."

"It's a false light, what you hope to see, not what is."

Detinna peered into the darkness around the Being. Its form kept trying to occupy the space she sought beyond it. Then the Being came into focus, and she was astonished by what she saw, or rather what she didn't see. It had no face. *No, I can't serve that, for it's something worse than death.*

Detinna was free, floating away, her dying not yet complete. Her consciousness felt like it was slipping away, as she was no longer attached to her body. The distance grew between her and the living. She could remain for a short while, as a ghost.

Detinna decided not to stay behind. She would find the tunnel of light and see what lay beyond. Maybe there was something, maybe not. And if there were, Delphi would join her there in time. She felt sadness for Delphi as he would grieve her, and she wondered what would become of him. She turned one fleeting glance and wished him well in life and love.

The hooded figure saw the foolish woman who tried to stop him and realized in an instant that his feast had doubled. He could not believe his good luck. He should wait, he knew, and preform the primary sacrifice. But she was helpless right in front of him. So he feasted. At that moment of high intoxication when her life passed, he was struck from behind by a surge of power. He instantly spun around, but this presence was already latched on. The more he tried to direct his power toward her, the more the witch drained his life force.

She had somehow guessed correctly his first response, to unleash his energy toward her. She had been able to redirect it, so that he was hit by both her attack and his response. It was fatal for his being in this world, and he shattered. The bits of him might regroup one day, but by then the cycle in the world would have passed. The Being, having no one to summon it, would search for another. It might take years, decades or centuries before a suitable candidate could be found. That did not bother him, but he would have to hide from the fury of the Being. It shouldn't be a problem, he thought, for the pieces of him were small and scattered.

CHAPTER XXI
THE NEW REGIME

"Are there any other orders, Prime Minister?"

Delphi glanced up from his desk to see Evak, impeccably dressed. He was alert, ready to carry his next order.

"You can go—no, wait a moment. I know that this is not exactly Presidential, but I've been wondering. Are you sure that things aren't being modified after I sign things into law?"

"Every i remains dotted, every t crossed. You know I can't control the entire bureaucracy or the informational world. And there are a number of ways to independently verify that things are done."

"And the popular support ... It is real?"

"You're riding a wave of popularity since we've had peace and with the new public works program."

"Still, aren't I a threat to various high-powered interests? Won't they one day succeed at removing me?"

"That's my job to prevent that, and I'm good at it."

"Are you satisfied with that? You well know that you could still become the Ruler."

"As you know, I'd rather not have that burden. I like remaining to the side and having some influence."

"It is lonely," Delphi sighed. "I'm amazed at how much we've been able to do. We've set a number of things in motion and dispersed considerable power. I'm only the First Minister now, not the Ruler. People are looking at me and the high officials not with fear but with expectation."

"Yes, remarkable progress has been made. And these measures will probably make the country and all of us last longer."

"Oh yes, they haven't found any trace of...." Delphi ended, unable to finish.

"Not so far, Mr. President. My guess remains that her body was transported to whatever lies beyond. We've questioned our own occult specialists who say as much."

Delphi paused for a few moments and considered his own mortality. "We've made some enemies who like to hasten our departure from this world."

"Yes, but we've handled them so far."

Delphi nodded and looked down at his papers. Usually, that was his signal to be left alone.

"May I venture," asked Evak, "is there something else that can be done? It's been almost a year now."

"No . . . nothing," said Delphi.

"Sir? There is one more thing."

"Yes," said Delphi, looking up with impatience. He did not want any therapeutic advice from his Head of Security.

"There is a need for a replacement for your personal security detail. And I – "

"Yes?" asked Delphi, wondering why this minor matter was being brought to his attention.

"We have a good choice. It's a woman...."

"You know I don't have any objection to a woman, if she's competent. I was guarded by a woman once, as you well know. And she protected me quite well from the power of the State."

"Sir, I would still like to bring her in for a brief interview, if possible. I'd like to make sure she's compatible...."

Delphi looked up. "Evak, I hope you're not trying to set me up. You know what happened to the prior Ruler."

The Head of Security remained stone faced, and Delphi waited a moment more before giving a nearly imperceptible nod. Evak left.

The next morning Delphi checked his calendar. There were dignitaries coming midmorning and a state dinner in the evening. A security briefing and some minor matters earlier in the morning.

The dossier for the security position was already lying on his desk. He didn't bother to open it. Of course, he trusted Evak's judgement. Or did he? Lately, he had replaced a couple Resistance veterans with former state security. Was he still keeping his options open?

With the dossier in his lap, Delphi swiveled his chair around to look out across the horizon, the gleaming skyscrapers, the aircars passing in the corridor. *Can I really continue to do this?* he wondered. *To be the Prime Minister and reform the empire? Nearly everyone said I was doing a good job so far. There have been three attempts on his life from far right-wing extremists, but they hadn't gotten very close. Still, I feel so alone.*

Delphi still grieved the loss of Detinna. He had allowed himself to grieve and resisted an easy way to help him forget. Any number of women in the empire would be willing to be his consort. But who could replace her? *She's gone forever...* he knew.

The door clicked. It must be the interviewee. Without turning around, Delphi said, "Have a seat."

He opened the dossier and examined the record briefly. Her service was in the Resistance, he noted favorably, but he spotted a gap in service. There had been no employment for several months. He wondered how the woman supported herself, for she had made no claim from the State. "You were out of commission for some time. Did something happen?" he asked, turning around, but still looking down.

"Yes," she answered firmly, without further elaboration.

Delphi felt a faint tingling. His mind flashed to the time he visited the tomb of Tiffany. It was a cold winter day, and the tomb appeared as if no one had ever visited it. He himself had been discouraged from visiting by Evak. Why would the Ruler visit the tomb of an obscure agent of the Resistance? Did they have an affair? It would not look good, he had said. Delphi, however, had insisted. It was cold, and he felt a chill. Evak was frowning. He couldn't keep the paparazzi from catching a long distance shot, that would soon be on the Tele across the empire.

Delphi had shed tears, and Evak consoled. "I read the files. She protected you well."

"Yes, she gave her life."

"Were you in love with her?" asked Evak.

Why had he thought to ask that? Delphi wondered. *Was he that transparent?* Of course, there were tears, for he couldn't hide his grief.

"I loved my wife and still do. But Tiffany saved my life more than once. I couldn't help becoming attached, but I wasn't unfaithful...."

"I understand," said Evak. "Is there anything more I can do?"

Delphi couldn't speak anymore.

He came back to the present. It couldn't be true.

"Delphi? You're the new head?" the woman questioned.

There was no doubt. A candidate, whom he didn't know, would not use his first name and have any hope of landing the job... unless it was her.

Delphi looked up at Tiffany and blurted out, "But you're dead. I visited your grave."

"Yes, I was dead, more or less at the time. But I revived, and the Resistance thought it useful for me to remain dead."

"How did you survive a direct hit?" asked Delphi, still not believing it was her. She looked much the same except there was a deepening of character in the face.

"It was a nearly direct hit and the beam pulse must have shorted some. Still, it should have killed me. I saw a path for me away, but I came back."

"There must have been someone to come back for?"

"Yes."

Of course. I spent all that time with her, and she hadn't talked about her lover. That's who must have cared for her during this time. Delphi decided not to pry. "Well, I am quite happy that you've survived. I can now thank you for saving my life more times than I can repay you. Tell me. What can I do for you?"

"That's not why I...." Her voice dropped off.

Well, there was some emotion at least after all our time together, Delphi realized. It helped ease his own pain.

Delphi looked again at the resume, but he couldn't read it. Didn't Evak know that they had a history. Was he trying to set him up, after all?

"I'm sorry. I can't give you this job," Delphi said, closing the portfolio.

Tiffany looked at him in the eye for a moment. Delphi returned her gaze, steady and penetrating.

"I can find some other position, of course, but not in the central office," Delphi offered. "You'll be well compensated. Evak will talk to you." He hit a button for him to enter.

Delphi looked back down, as if examining other papers, but he heard no sign of Tiffany leaving. He couldn't bring himself to repeat himself. He was the Prime Minister. He only needed to say things once.

Evak entered the room just then, and Delphi glanced up.

Tiffany was still in her chair, her head down, tears streaming down her face.

Delphi suddenly understood.

Evak spoke. "I'm sorry, sir. I thought . . . I knew that she had a prior—my apologies, sir.... I will escort her out immediately."

"No, Evak, that won't be necessary. We need a moment more...."

"Sir . . . the delegation is outside waiting."

"I'm able to leave now," said Tiffany, rising. "You needn't do anything more for me."

Tiffany's calm, composed demeanor had returned. *What strength,* thought Delphi.

She was already stepping away when Delphi called out, "Please, wait."

Tiffany turned, almost against her will. One did not regard the request of the Head of State lightly. Still, it was a request, she felt, and not an order.

"I'm having dinner with some dignitaries tonight. Sometimes their conversation gets stale, and I wouldn't mind an old friend sitting next to me. I have precious few of those."

"Well, I...." Tiffany began. She looked to Evak, who showed surprise, and gave a slight nod.

"Why yes, I supposed I can...."

"You can also bring a special friend if you want. I don't want you to have to put up with just me and the dignitaries."

"Well sir, there's no one else that...."

Delphi smiled. He had guessed right. "No need to call me sir. Delphi will do fine."

Evak inserted. "Sir, you're seriously behind schedule."

"Alright," said Delphi. "You can see who I obey around here."

Delphi paused a moment, then hugged Tiffany.

Tiffany returned the hug, her eyes holding surprise.

A moment later, the First Minster was gone.

Evak turned to Tiffany and said, "Ms. Nelson, there will be a car and an assistant for you waiting outside in five minutes. The assistant can help with whatever preparations you might need for tonight. May I escort you out?"

"Evak, that won't be necessary. I know my way out."

"I insist. It's my pleasure," returned Evak.

EPILOG

Dr. Burgess heard the ring of the Time Expansion center. He was planning a vacation, which he had hoped to be a week, but he could only afford a weekend. His new secretary, Gennell, knocked on his door. "Two new retreatants – a couple with an infant – are here. I tried to tell them no infants can attend retreats, but they acted like that didn't matter. They also had a couple of friends, hovering around outside, so they must be important people. They say they're interested in time expansion."

"Well, have them wait in the foyer and serve them some tea."

"Sir, I noticed there are a few aircars that have been there since early this morning. I hope you're not in any special trouble with the State."

"No, no. I'm not expecting in problems now. Our books are clean."

"Are you sure? They can always find something. I know you said you have friends in high places, but you've never bothered to call on them. I hope you won't have to call on them now."

"The retreatants are probably just some wealthy people with connections. Don't worry. We take both high and low. Did you review the guidelines and payment?"

"Sir, they've already written out a check for some ungodly amount. You won't have any trouble making payroll and you'll even be able to take that week-like vacation to St. Thomas."

"Didn't you explain to them that payment is only given after the workshop, after they are satisfied? No exceptions."

"They insisted, sir. And you know we could really use this now."

"Alright, Gennell, let me handle it from here."

"One more thing. They're insisting on a course this very weekend. I told them that you're planning to be away. I don't know what you want to do, but—"

"That won't be necessary. I'll talk to them myself. I'm sure that it's not the only weekend they're available."

Dr. Burgess was surprised to see that the perspective retreatants were Delphi and Tiffany. Over tea there were happy exchanges and much catching up on events and family. Dr. Burgess had married his assistant, Alice, and he had a child as well.

After sharing personal matters, they recollected the last days of the empire.

"Cross our fingers," said Dr. Burgess. "There's a rumor that the Being is attempting to regroup. We must remain vigilant."

"Especially me," said Delphi. " Every day, I think about ways to give out power."

Then Delphi thought to say, "I'm sorry it's taken this long of a time to see you, although I know you prefer to keep a low profile. We're so glad to have some real time free."

"Yes. It's important to be a bit on the outside. But about this weekend," said Dr. Burgess, holding the check. "I'm sorry but I can't—"

"I insist," said Delphi. "And I know you're planning a vacation this coming weekend. We're hoping that you might like to have some company."

"Vacations are the best for time expansion," added Tiffany. "And I would really like to meet Alice."

"Why yes, of course, maybe—if you don't mind roughing it. We were going to camp out. Let me check with my wife. I'm sure she'd be delighted."

"If you don't mind, we'd like to go for a full week and to St. Thomas instead."

"Why, that was what we originally planned. Wait—how did you know? I suppose that you have ways of finding things out," said Dr.

Burgess, casting an eye at his secretary, who was acting as if she wasn't listening so intently.

"Expenses for the trip are already taken care of," said Tiffany. "That's part of the security arrangement."

"Well, what can I say?" said Dr. Burgess. "Still, I really can't accept this check now. I've never deviated from policy, so why start now. Not until after the course is finished and you're satisfied."

"If I'm not mistaken, I think I owe money for past services," said Delphi. "The Time Expansion course that got us mixed up in all this. It's not always been easy, but I'm satisfied with services rendered. And I can set the price. Isn't that the policy too?"

"Why yes. But that was some time ago, and things have taken many turns...."

"So we're in agreement. As for the vacation, consider that a bonus."

"You can give a few tips on Time Expansion on the trip if you like," added Tiffany.

"You don't leave me much of a choice," said Dr. Burgess, mulling.

"I'll deposit this today," said his secretary, taking the check out of Dr. Burgess's hand.

Delphi seemed to wink to the secretary, and Dr. Burgess was left wondering as the two departed.

Later that day, Dr. Burgess asked Gennell, "Did you have something to do with this?"

"I'll own up," said Gennell, who couldn't stop from beaming. "You said you had friends in high places. So I did some research about past clients and came across someone named Delphi. I placed a call and was surprised that I was directed to the new President."

"You were able to reach the President like that? And I can't believe that you told him about our situation and asked for money!"

"I just told him how things were. You know, he was curious and asked a lot of questions. He sounded like he really wanted to see you too."

"I see," said Dr. Burgess, still looking displeased.

"I know it was a big breach in protocol, but if I had asked for permission, you wouldn't have agreed."

"That's true, Gennell. Can you bring me your employment contract?"

"My contract?"

"Yes, I want to add some new duties and give you a raise."

The End

Did you love *The Resistance & the Empire*? Then you should read *Twelve Suspects*[1] by Michael A. Susko!

The Roman emperor is fearful of a Delphic oracle which states that "From the bones of twelve, a phoenix shall rise that will rule Rome." An imperial investigator is sent to determine the paradoxical threat to Rome--to find the twelve and where they hid the missing bones of their founder. Their disappearances resolve into bones and a surprise murder mystery. Read this work to place yourself in the first century where oracles, bones, and small groups can shake the foundations of empire.

Read more at https://www.allroneofus.com/.

---

1. https://books2read.com/u/bwadlG

2. https://books2read.com/u/bwadlG

Also by Michael A. Susko

The Dreaming Series
Sleek Back
Streak and Cave Bear Dreaming
Moby and Marsupial Mole Dreaming

The Dream World Trilogy
Delphi, the Time Thief, and the Dream World
Detinna and the Cave God
The Resistance & the Empire

Worlds to the Side
Down Below and the Archon's Castle
Up Above and the Runaway
Across the Gulf and Journey Into Un-Time
On the Bay and a Wild Child Found
In the Wild and Do One Wild Thing
On the Mountain and Two Are Missing
To the Beginning and Journey Through Here

The Generation of LIfe: Imagery, Ritual and Experiences in Deep
Caves
Alwon in Another World: An Archetypal Voyage
Line In the Wall
Twelve Suspects

Watch for more at https://www.allroneofus.com/.

About the Author

In this book, the author combines his work leading groups of dream interpretation, with his study of empires and their generational course, for which he has given conference presentations. In this third part of trilogy, he imagines how behind-the scene psychic battles, involving ordinary people, influence the course of history.

Read more at https://www.allroneofus.com/.